SUSANNAH SCREAMING

Also by Carolyn Weston
Poor, Poor, Ophelia
Rouse the Demon

SUSANNAH
SCREAMING

A KRUG & KELLOG THRILLER

CAROLYN WESTON

Text copyright © 2015 Brash Books LLC
All rights reserved.

ISBN: 1941298508
ISBN 13: 9781941298503

Published by Brash Books, LLC
12120 State Line #253,
Leawood, Kansas 66209

www.brash-books.com

ONE

"This is KCOP," announced the gentle disembodied FM voice. "Kay-cop, your Santa Monica station." Bringing the best in music. And five minutes of news. Every hour on the hour.

What sounded like theme music floated from the hidden speakers. Yawning, leaning back against the pink-enameled Maytag which spun his meager wash, Rees tried to identify the melody, but he could not. The washer pulsed warmly against his buttocks. Felt good, he decided. My friend, the machine. Lovable laundromats for lonely hearts.

"Four o'clock," the radio was telling him portentously. Weather would be fine in Southern California this Monday morning, but with low coastal fog night and morning. The news was the usual collection of catastrophes. Then the music continued, bland as Muzak, almost as comforting as sleep. Insomniacs' delight, Rees thought. Anything was better than silence at four in the morning, even this mindless burble of electronic sound which probably ran night and day here, along with the gas dryers, the rows of washers, the water heaters hissing and humming like benign monsters behind a pink-painted partition.

His laundry had five minutes more on its cycle. Lighting a cigarette, he wandered down the long, narrow washing-machine-lined storefront and looked out the plate-glass display window at the dark street. Montana Avenue. He had noticed the name

1

and this twenty-four-hour laundromat when he had passed by yesterday.

At this hour the street was dark and deserted, a ghost-town thoroughfare. Across the way was a garden and florist shop. On this side, across the alley beside the laundromat, was the liquor store and market where he had shopped yesterday for the scotch and soda, the cheese and crackers, which were his version of a spinster's tea and toast.

On the dark pane, his own reflection peered back at him, dim and transparent, like a photo negative held up to bad light. No mistaking that image, he thought bleakly. The loner. Behind his eyes throbbed the slow ache of constant fatigue which had become chronic in the last eighteen months, for he had lost the habit of sleep. Even his bones were tired. Self-pity had become a fearful problem.

But the face which looked back at him was not pitying. A sallow, dark-browed Celtic visage—the face of a fanatic, Ellen had once said. He had laughed at the time. But he'd been happy then.

The washing machine clicked off behind him. Simultaneously the rumble of the hidden water heaters lessened, and as Rees dug his steamy heap of clothing out of the washer, he could hear a droning far off. A summer sound. Like bees in a garden. It grew louder and louder while he tossed his laundry into one of the dryers standing open like a flimsy old-fashioned safe, the somnolent hum becoming a mechanical roar—a motorcycle approaching at high speed. And now he could hear a car also, perhaps a block behind. A chase? he wondered. Cops and robbers. Diverted, Rees slammed the dryer shut. But he forgot the nickels which made it go.

For sudden light flared across the front window of the laundromat. He caught a fleeting glimpse of the lunatic shadow crouched behind the single headlamp as the motorcycle screeched into the alley, booming by the building so violently that the front panes shivered. Christ, at that speed, the fool *had* to skid. Idiot,

2

idiot. He heard the cycle reeling out of control and rushed for the back door of the laundromat which let into a parking area beside the alley. But he wasn't quick enough. The clang and clatter of ripping metal and breaking glass resounded down the alley. But the vacuumlike moment of silence which follows wrecks was drowned out by the car which rocked diagonally, tires howling, across Montana and into the alley. Jumping back, Rees had a glimpse of a sedan, an impression of a driver, something glittering in the back seat. The wind of the big dark car's passage swirled dust back into his face as he stopped in the middle of the alley—spectator, then participant, in another swift and terrible nightmare:

The car hit the wrecked motorcycle, and in the sheeting glare of its headlights channeled up the fenced alley like light in a tunnel, he saw metallic debris flying, and behind that, at the dim edges of illumination, a hunched, crippled figure running. Then the car lights went out. Paralyzed, his mind rejecting what his senses perceived, Rees watched the shadowy vehicle swerve left, then right, then left again, hunting as impersonally as a missile on target. An instant later, he heard the impact, solid yet soft. The car stopped, then backed up. Howling *"No"* or *"Stop"*—he would never remember—Rees pounded up the alley. But the car went on, jolting as if it rode over an abandoned tire. And at the next street north it turned left, roaring away. Rees bent over the dark figure crumpled like a ragbag bundle. The motorcyclist was dead. Even in the dark there was no mistaking that life was crushed out of him.

Later, he found out that a neighbor had heard the crash, his shouting, and instead of investigating, had called the police. Rees was still crouched by the body when he heard the siren. A prowl car turned up the alley off Montana. And as the police car pulled up, back gates in the tall fencing began to open. Rees was surrounded suddenly by robed and slippered spectators whose avid faces, pasty in the headlights, seemed ghostly counterparts of those others…Hovering over him like merciless masks as he held Ellen. Hovering while he watched her die…

The patrolmen moved in. And as they bent over the body, Rees moved back, leaning shakily against the fence. He could hardly breathe as he told them. He knew he sounded hysterical, but it did not occur to him that they might not believe him until he heard the one who radioed for an ambulance calling what happened "a hit-and-run." The other kept talking to the spectators about "the accident."

"But it wasn't," Rees kept saying hoarsely. "Don't you understand what I've been saying?"

"Take it easy, mister," the policeman who had been radioing said soothingly.

"It wasn't hit-and-run. That car chased him—"

"We'll take down your statement in a minute, mister. Just take it easy." The policeman glanced around the crowd, professionally calm and rational. "Anybody else see or hear this car?"

"All I heard was a crash and him yelling, Officer." Tubby in his bathrobe, his bald head gleaming, one of the neighbors peered curiously at Rees. "Yelling something, I don't know what it was. Then I heard the siren, so I come out to have a look—"

"You're the one who called in, then?"

"That's right, Officer." He pursed his lips self-importantly. "Another time, I might of come out first, see if I could help any. But not these days. You got to—"

"I saw the car," a soft female voice beyond the light interrupted him. Separating like a stage crowd, the bystanders let her through—a young woman wearing a trench coat many sizes too large for her. She was smiling nervously and kept her head turned away to avoid seeing the body. "At the other end of the alley." She was pointing north where the car had disappeared. "It turned into the street just as I came around the corner."

"What kind of a car, miss?"

She blinked at the policeman and he smiled encouragingly. She was a very pretty girl in her early twenties, tallish, obviously slender under the too-large coat. "Well, a sedan, I think. But it was going so fast—"

"You notice the color, or what make it was?"

"Green, I think. Dark green."

"It was black," Rees said. "A black Mercedes."

"You see a Mercedes too, miss?"

"Well, no, actually." She glanced at Rees, then away again. "Didn't look like an import to me."

"All right," the patrolman said before Rees could protest, "we'll get both your statements later. Miss, if you'd like to sit in the car over here," and he led her away.

Rees realized the policeman meant to separate them. But from the girl's pleased, half-flirtatious attitude, it was obvious she thought it was courtesy. Why had she claimed the car was green? he wondered. And she hadn't said whether she had been driving or walking when she saw it. Doubt filled him suddenly, a dizzy aftermath of his blinding shock. At the center of his mind, Ellen's face burned incandescent...Eyes closed. Chalky white. They marked DOA on her pale forehead...Sickening, Rees leaned against the fence again. Maybe the car had been green after all.

Another patrol car arrived, then another. After what seemed an eternity, an ambulance rolled up the alley, its siren a dying moan. Then a pale-colored Mustang pulled up, and two men got out. One of the patrolmen pointed to Rees and they made a beeline for him—detectives, they told him. The older of the two said, "You're the eyewitness, right?"

Rees nodded, stumbling slightly when the older one took his arm, leading him over to the Mustang.

"Patrolman who called in said you're claiming this wasn't an accident."

"Look, I know what I saw!" Trembling, Rees leaned against the Mustang. "That car chased him, and caught him—"

"All right, mister, we're not arguing with you. Just trying to find out what happened."

The young one opened one of the Mustang's two doors, pulling the seat forward. "How about sitting inside while we talk," he suggested mildly. "Be more comfortable for you."

Rees climbed shakily into the back seat. Both detectives sat in the front with their legs out the open doors. Suddenly aware of the dome light shining on his face, of the fact that he couldn't get out now unless they let him, Rees felt a clutch of remembered terror. The older one was asking for identification, and fumbling, Rees pulled his driver's license out of his wallet, handing it over the back of the front seat.

"Paul Joseph Rees, hah? San Francisco." The older one's weatherbeaten face creased into a smile, but his eyes looked hard as marbles, cold and watchful. "You still live at this address in Frisco, Mr. Rees?"

"Not any longer. I don't have a permanent address as yet."

"Sounds like you're planning on locating down here." The young one was smiling, too. A real smile. "Welcome to Southern California."

Relaxing slightly, Rees fixed his attention on the pleasant unlined face. What had he said his name was? Detective Somebody. About twenty-five, deeply tanned, a real Southern California type, with his big shoulders and sun-bleached brown hair—one of the sun worshipers. The other one's name was Krug, and it suited him. A sergeant. And a bastard, Rees thought. "How about—" He was croaking, he realized, and cleared his throat. "How about some coffee? There's a vending machine in the laundromat. Don't know about you, but I could use a lift."

"Good idea," Detective Somebody agreed.

But the older one couldn't be had that easily. "Your company transfer you, something like that, Mr. Rees?"

"I don't have a company."

"That mean you're unemployed?"

"That's right." Rees swallowed dryness. "Look, I don't quite see what this has to do with my being a witness here—"

"Take it easy, Mr. Rees, we're just doing our job like always." Krug eyed him calmly. "What's your line of work?"

"I'm a chemist."

"Sounds good." Krug sucked his teeth. "You been out of work long?"

The lie came facilely: "Only a couple of weeks. I decided to take a vacation, then relocate down here."

"Where you staying, Mr. Rees?"

"At the Pelican Motel. It's on the oceanfront."

"Couple hundred feet above it, you mean." Krug grinned. "Top of the palisades. Ocean Avenue, right?" Without waiting for corroboration, he went on: "So you been in town—what?—a week or so?"

"No, only since Friday."

"Friday. Un-hunh. Okay, Mr. Rees, let's hear your story."

He told it again, but this time the words seemed stale, exaggerated. Some element was missing, he realized. Lying had somehow destroyed his certainty.

The young one kept writing in a notebook, but the older one simply sat there staring at Rees until he had finished talking. Then after a reflective silence he said, "That all of it?"

Bastard cop. "Yes, I think that's everything."

Krug sighed gustily. "No details then, I guess. Like a license number. What the driver looked like."

"Sorry. It all happened so fast, you see. But maybe that girl—"

"Sure." Krug cut him off. "Okay, Mr. Rees." He slid off the seat, and, standing outside the car, bent to look in. "Better be sure," he advised quietly. "Know what I mean? What you're talking about here is homicide."

"Yes, I realize—"

"Okay. All I meant was, you sign a statement, it's official, get me?" Then he walked away.

"What the hell is he trying to do?"

"Easy, Mr. Rees, it's all part of our job." The young detective was smiling again. "We only want to make sure you know what you're saying." He snapped his notebook shut and glanced at his watch. "We'll probably be here awhile. Why don't you go get that cup of coffee you were talking about? Then we'll be ready to write up a witness statement for your signature."

No wonder people don't cooperate with the police. "Do I have any choice?" Rees asked.

"Afraid not," the young detective said cheerfully. "See you later, okay?" And he followed his partner up the alley.

Rees wandered back into the laundromat and, warmed by a Styrofoam cup of vending-machine coffee, broodingly watched his laundry tumbling inside the barrel of the dryer. He wished now he had never got involved. Much later it occurred to him that the driver of that Mercedes must be wishing the same.

TWO

"Nice pair of night crawlers we got for witnesses," Al Krug commented sourly when they had finished with the girl. "I'll believe that guy's a chemist when I see his diploma. As for her—" He made a flatulent sound with his lips. "All that crap about insomnia. For my dough, she was probably hoofing it home from her last trick."

Her name was Susannah Roche, the girl had told them, and she lived in one of the high-rise apartment buildings on Ocean Avenue. "I'm an actress," she had added brightly, snuggling down into the trench coat. "And no cracks, please. Because I really am. Call the Guild if you don't believe me…"

The uniformed patrolman sitting in the front seat of the squad car grinned appreciatively, and she beamed at him. Then catching Krug's look, she assumed an exaggeratedly serious expression. "Couldn't sleep," she went on, "and I get buggy trying to count sheep. So I took myself a walk, same as I do lots of nights. Or did till tonight. Now that I realize people get murdered—" She shivered theatrically. "Probably have nightmares for weeks." She turned to Krug. "Was he really run down on purpose? I mean, it seems such a *crazy* way to *kill* somebody! Like a schlock movie or something." She hesitated. "Couldn't that man—" Then she stopped herself. "Forget I said that. Let's face it, who'd tell a nut story like that if it wasn't true? You'd have to be freaking out—"

"You let us worry about that." Impatiently, Krug blew out his breath. "Go on, Miss Roche, let's try to get this thing moving."

"Well, I was walking up Fourteenth Street, and when I was almost at the corner, I heard this noise. Like a crash or something. So, instead of heading home, I turned right. What is it— east? Anyway, I turn the corner on Alta, and this car comes— *varoom!*—out of the alley."

"You see the driver?"

"Not really. But it was a man, I think."

"Anybody else in the car?"

"Not that I could see."

"And the car was a dark-green sedan, you think?"

"That's right."

"Not a Mercedes."

She hesitated again. "Well—you dig—I'm very visual. Most theater people are. We develop this sense of—"

"Miss Roche," Krug said warningly, "let's get to it."

"What I'm talking about is this picture in my mind."

"An impression," Casey Kellog, Krug's partner, suggested.

"Something like that." She smiled at him brilliantly. "Detroit wheels, anyway. One of the medium ones. Like a Camaro, maybe."

"Any impression"—Krug came down hard on the word—"of anything like a license number?"

"Oh, wow," she groaned, "come *on*, man. It was there and gone"—snapping her fingers—"just like that!"

"Then what did you do?"

"Me? What did *I* do?" As she peered at his partner, her large, glistening gray eyes widening, Casey realized she might be nearsighted. Some witness, he thought wearily. "If you mean," she was saying, "did I walk down this spookville alley, you're dreaming! I didn't move till I saw the cop—the police car. But I kept having this freaky feeling. Like something terrible had happened—"

"Apprehension," Casey said.

"Right on." Another melting smile transformed her into a beauty. "Anyway, I heard the siren. So I kept waiting. And when I saw the lights down the alley..."

Knowing they would have another chance at both witnesses, they hadn't wasted any more time on Susannah Roche. Krug told her that she would be driven to police headquarters, where her statement would be typed for signature, and climbed out of the squad car. Casey followed him. As they walked up the alley her clear complaining voice echoed after them: she didn't have all night, et cetera. Witnesses never had any time, it seemed.

Krug peered in through the open doors of the ambulance where a medical man in wrinkled whites was strapping the body in. "You guys all set to roll?"

"Just about, Al." He tossed Krug a wallet. "Here's his ID. Pictures and taping're all done. I'll log whatever else is in his pockets. Good sleuthing, gents!" He pulled the doors closed.

Holding the wallet up into the glare of a squad-car spotlight, Krug examined the driver's license with its photo of a bearded, long-haired young man wearing metal-framed *Easy Rider* glasses. "All these dudes look alike," he muttered. "Name's Gerald Hower Barrett. Address could be Ocean Park." He opened the money compartment. "Some bills here." Then he whistled through his teeth. "A pile of twenties. Prosperous dude, right?" He pocketed the wallet. "Okay, let's save the neighbors here for the daylight boys to wrap up. Give 'em something to get started on."

They went on to the lab van parked beyond the ambulance. Two technicians Casey recognized were squatting near the wreckage of the motorcycle inspecting a twisted red-painted cycle fender. "Got a make on your hit-and-runner's color, maybe," the gray-haired one—McGregor—reported. "Black, looks like."

"Score one for our so-called chemist." With his hands in his pockets, Krug rocked on his heels. "What you say, sport?" he asked Casey. "Think that sexy broad's playing some kind of a game here?"

Casey grinned. "Think she might need glasses, Al."

"Jesus, some witness." He peered at the scrap of metal McGregor was holding. "Looks like black to me."

"I'd say so." McGregor nodded. "We'll test for hue and paint type when we get back to the lab. Got some glass here, too." He patted the plastic-covered evidence box sitting at his feet. "Pieces of headlight. From the amount, I'd say your hit-and-runner probably lost a lamp, too."

"Any tire marks?" Krug asked.

"You're kidding. On this?" McGregor spat into the alley. "Look at that. Dust with asphalt paving underneath. Not a chance in a million of a clear cast." Then he winked at Casey. "How you like night tour, young fella? Pretty rough on a horny young bachelor, hah?"

"Don't worry about him," Krug grunted. "He's probably fixed up already with an afternoon chick."

"No such luck." Casey sighed. "Although I appreciate the thought. How soon can you tell us about the paint, Mac?"

McGregor looked at his partner. "Couple hours, maybe?"

Dourly the other man nodded. "Glass'll take longer."

"Okay," Krug said, "see you guys later," and still talking, he started back down the alley, not bothering to look to see if Casey was following. "Let's collect our witnesses and get back. The sooner we get the paperwork done, the sooner day watch can hit this guy Barrett's pad. Maybe they'll find something there we can really go to work on." The eternal hope of the detective.

THREE

Driving his own Volkswagen, Rees followed the Mustang through the early-morning grayness. He was surprised when the detectives ahead stopped for traffic signals at Wilshire Boulevard and again at a street named Colorado. You never think of policemen as having to obey ordinary laws. Once, a moony face looked briefly back at him through the Mustang's rear window—the girl, he realized. Of course they would want her official statement also. Green American-made sedan versus black Mercedes. Conflicting witnesses. Oh hell, he thought exhaustedly, what's the difference? The police would need a miracle to find anybody to prosecute.

A Sears store reeled by on his left, then Rees followed the Mustang south across a bridge over the Santa Monica Freeway. Ahead lay a series of white stucco public buildings. In front of the first one, he saw a lighted sign at the curb—*Police Station*—marking an entrance. The Mustang swung in and disappeared behind the building. Rees followed, and, parking his car among official vehicles in the lot, joined the detectives and the girl as they entered the brightly lighted Police Department housed like a nerve center behind the Santa Monica City Hall.

"This way," Krug said. Beefy in his baggy slacks and a sports coat which had seen better days, he led them along a shiny corridor and up a flight of stairs. Passing a door marked "Juvenile" in the narrow hall at the top, they entered the Detective Bureau—a large, light squad room with a counter in the front, rows of desks behind, most of which were empty at this hour. "Grab a seat,"

Krug told them. "We'll run over what you folks gave us, then type it up for you to sign, okay?"

The younger one was pulling up a straight chair from a neighboring desk for the girl. Krug settled with a grunt into a swivel chair. Sitting on either side of his desk, Rees and the girl waited as he leaned back watching while his partner perched on the corner of the desk and opened his notebook, leafing through it.

The young one kept swallowing huge yawns, Rees noticed, and his tanned face looked tired now, washed out under the cold pervasive light which filled the big office. Doesn't look like a cop, he thought. Twenty years and he will, though. The young detective began to read slowly from his notes, and like a palimpsest superimposed over the present scene, Rees saw himself that other time: sitting like this with his fury dead in him, his spirit drowned in another man's blood while a detective read back his own words...*I, Paul Joseph Rees, do hereby confess of my own free will and in full cognizance of what I am saying, that I assaulted with intent to do bodily injury—*

"Mr. Rees," Krug's voice recalled him sharply.

"Sorry," he mumbled. "I didn't get—"

"We were asking if you've ever had any experience with the police before."

A mind reader. Spellbound, Rees stared at him. "Why, no," he managed to say finally. "No, of course not."

"No offense intended." Krug was smiling faintly, his cold eyes watchful. "Lots of people who've never even had a traffic ticket have dealings with the police. Anyhow," he added in a mild tone which was somehow chilling, "I was asking you both. Miss Roche, too. Just in case you didn't understand you could be subpoenaed from now on."

Unable to trust himself, Rees only nodded. He was certain that the conversational trap he had fallen into was deliberate, a cop trick. Even the young one seemed to look at him differently now. Once a con, always a con. Tempted to walk out, Rees restrained himself, knowing that he would only be furnishing a bullyboy like Krug with further fuel.

The girl was watching him too, he saw, slumped and huddled like a waif inside the huge trench coat. A man's coat, he recognized vaguely. Husband's? Boyfriend's? She had turned up the sleeves, exposing the coat's faded yellow-and-black plaid lining. One of the sleeves, which exaggerated the delicacy of her wrists and ringless hands, had a peculiar triangle-shaped tear in the lining. Her nails looked like pale opalescent shells. Under the too-long, ridiculous raincoat, her purple ankle-strapped platform shoes looked like part of a musical comedy costume.

As if she knew how absurd she looked, she made a face at Rees, a droll secretive grimace which included him in some joke on herself. Or perhaps on both of them, he decided. She was trapped in this oppressive officialdom too, and perhaps finding it almost as much of a strain.

Smiling back at her, he felt the stir of some awareness in himself, a lost sense of the possibility of happiness coming to life like a half-severed nerve. With a girl like this, you could laugh and be carefree, he thought. The idea filled him with such longing and pleasure that he went dizzy for a second. When we're through here, he decided, I'll ask her to have breakfast with me. And he knew if he did, and she accepted, he would probably take it as an omen. He was hungry for signs, famished now, he realized, for some glimpse of the future. He had lived too long in an emotional wasteland.

FOUR

"Well, thanks to Mr. Clean washing his clothes at four in the morning, looks like we got ourselves a homicide," Krug said. "And for my dough it smells from here to tomorrow. That Rees dude's as phony as a three-dollar bill."

The witnesses were waiting at the other end of the squad room for their statements to be typed. Casey studied Paul Rees for a moment. A tired man. Perhaps thirty. Lean and lanky, morose-looking. Was it an old cop hunch that made Krug suspect him, he wondered—or just his usual prejudice against anyone younger? "Seems all right to me, Al," he said neutrally. "Shaky, sure, but who wouldn't be?"

"He'd be a hell of a lot shakier without that girl to back him up."

"I didn't mean—"

"I know what you meant! All I'm saying is, without her, we'd have to play him maybe for kinky with a story like that. As it is—" He sucked his teeth, staring in space, his ruddy face sour as usual. "Well, let's let it lay for now. But when we get through with the openers, I'm checking out that dude, but fast."

There wasn't time to file a report before Lieutenant Timms came on duty, so they filled him in verbally. "Sounds crazy, all right," he commented. "Your witnesses still around?"

Krug shook his head. "Signed and gone. You just missed 'em."

"Doesn't hurt my feelings." Timms chewed his lower lip. "Think your eyewitness is solid, Al?"

"I'd feel a hell of a lot better if he was a local."

Timms's tufty eyebrows lifted. Rubbing his freshly shaved jaw, he looked at Casey. "You got qualms, too?"

"No, sir. He seemed solid enough to me."

"How about this woman? Susannah Whatshername."

"A hooker—what else?" Krug grunted. "But at least she's local."

"You've got local on the brain this morning, Al. What's eating you?"

"A feeling, that's all. Something about that guy Rees just don't strike me as kosher. Too nervous, maybe—I don't know. Can't put my finger on anything positive yet."

"All right, check him out. No use beating our brains if he's a nut of some kind. Anything from the lab yet?"

"Not so far. We got a Telex off to Washington. The usual. Just in case there's no make on any kinfolk where Barrett lives. The rest"—Krug yawned and stretched like a bear—"up to you day-watch dudes. Me, I'm ready for about eight hours solid."

"Not a chance, Al. With two guys out sick and one on vacation—"

Krug groaned. "Okay, so what's next, we hit Barrett's pad?"

Timms nodded. "By the time you get back, we ought to have the prelim and something from the lab…"

" 'Be a policeman,' " Casey quoted as they pounded down the stairs. " 'Serve your fellow man'—"

"Bullshit. Nobody but the ass end of a donkey stays a cop anymore. The smart guys all get out into the rackets. You got Barrett's address handy?"

Casey fished out his notebook for Krug, and started the Mustang, pulling out onto Main. Krug was licking his thumb to turn pages—a habit that nauseated Casey. "You were right, Al, it's got to be Ocean Park. Just off Neilson, I think."

"Real class address, yeah." Krug read it off. Then scowling out the window as they swung right onto Pico, catching the signal left at Neilson, he made his usual comment. "Christ, look at the shacks around here. They ought to tear down the whole god-dam district."

After a few blocks, Casey turned right again, driving slowly along a narrow side street lined with shabby old beach cottages crammed together on small lots. The front-stoop sitters were already out, he saw—old men in too-large hats and baggy pants. An elderly woman with black-dyed hair and sparkle-rimmed glasses stared after them with the unabashed curiosity of the foreigner. Beyond the roofs of the old houses the sea seemed to curve bowl-like upward, melting into the low early-morning fog.

"Oh-Sheeny Park," Krug groused. "A truckload of kerosene and a box of matches is what this place needs. There it is." He pointed. "That motel-type joint."

Casey pulled up in front of a peeling one-story stucco—obviously several units, probably one room and bath each—with a walk down the side leading to each door. In a cluster near the back stood four or five motorcycles of various makes.

"Dig the wheels. Want to bet this is one of those hogger joints?" Krug blew out his breath. "Christ, all we need to really start this thing right is a pack of mouthy two-bit Hell's Angels types."

Knife carriers, Casey thought. Chain wielders. Weary as he was of his partner's constant griping, this time he had to agree with him.

"Am I *glad* to be *out* of there!" He heard her sigh beside him. "That older one really bugged me. Sourpuss. Didn't he give you the creeps?"

"Not particularly," Rees lied. "A policeman is a policeman is a policeman."

"You putting me on?" She turned in the narrow front seat, knees touching his thigh. Her long, silky dark-brown hair blew across her face like a torn veil. Impatiently, she pushed it back. "Man, are you trying to tell me he didn't *scare* you?"

"Don't be silly." He cleared his throat. "Sorry. Why should he scare me?"

"Guilt, man, guilt. The human condition."

She was smiling, he saw. Not serious? He couldn't be sure.

"So who isn't spooked around cops," she was saying in a wry tone. "*I* always get the feeling they've got X-ray eyes. You smoke too much," she added abruptly. "That's what's wrong with your throat. And you know what's going to happen? Cancer and out. Bye-bye, Mr. American Pie."

"Thank you for the diagnosis, Doctor. Now having made my day, do you think you can direct me to the nearest beanery?"

"No problem, there's one two blocks from here." She pointed ahead. "Just follow your nose. My dad used to say that. We were always following our noses." She giggled. "Mostly into trouble, I seem to recall."

Intensely aware of her, Rees gunned the Volkswagen, grinding the gears. *You trying to tell me he didn't scare you?* Wondering if Krug could have noticed anything, he felt a lessening of delight like a cloud on his spirit. "What makes you think he scared me?" he asked as casually as he could when they had stopped for a signal and he could watch her expression.

"Well, let me see." She frowned consideringly. "Would you believe something psychic—like woman's intuition?"

Rees suppressed a sigh. "Please, I'd really like to know."

"The light's green again."

The Volkswagen shot forward.

"See that sign that says Norm's?"

"I see it." He had forgotten how exasperating women could be.

"Jesus, you dudes really hit it early!" He kept yawning hugely, puffing foul breaths at them through the three inches open between the doorframe and the chain-held door marked *Manager*. "You know what time it is?"

"So sorry," Krug apologized sarcastically. "Maybe next time something happens to one of your tenants, we can arrange it better for your beauty sleep. Which one is Barrett's place?"

"Number Six. Last door at the end."

Krug waited, staring at the bleary eye, the puffy cheek, the portion of wiry-bearded chin, which were all they could see of the manager's face. "You going to open up for us?" he asked finally.

"Not without a paper I ain't."

Krug sighed. "So we get a warrant. Takes an hour, maybe more, and we got to wait for it. Judges like their sleep, too. You want to waste the taxpayers' money with all that?"

"Fuck the goddam taxpayers, I ain't letting nobody—" His voice rose in a yelp as Krug reached in swiftly, grabbing a handful of beard. "Leggo me!"

"You got one minute, asshole."

"That's police brutality, and I got a witness in here!" He yelped again as Krug twisted tighter.

"Tell Witness to get decent, because you're opening up—like now, right?"

Tearing, the one eye glared out at them. Then the manager nodded, grimacing with pain. Krug let him go and he closed the door. As the chain rattled out of its slot, they could hear whispering, then the manager's howl: "You heard him, for Chrissake! Come on, will ya? Get your butt in that bathroom!"

Krug grinned at Casey. "Any bets?" he asked softly as bedsprings twanged behind the door. "Easy as anything it could be another guy. That *macho* beard don't fool me any."

Good old Uncle Al, your friendly neighborhood psychologist. Casey shook his head—no bets—yawning so hard his jaw cracked. Then watery-eyed, he watched the door swing open, wide this time.

"Okay, you mothers." The bearded manager was yanking a wrinkled robe around a body shaped like a beer barrel. "I'm opening the goddam door, but that's all I'm doing. Better believe I'm putting in a complaint, too!"

"Drop by Fingerprinting while you're at it," Krug suggested. "They'll probably be real glad to check out a citizen like you."

Number Six was heavily draped, cave-black after the misty glare outside. Casey fumbled for and found the light switch by the door. Blinking in the glaring overhead illumination common in such places, they silently surveyed the chaos of search or sudden departure—bureau drawers hanging open, an Army-style footlocker turned upside down in the middle of the floor, unmade tumbled bed, closet standing open.

"Looks like somebody beat us here," Krug commented.

"A real trash job." Casey nodded. "Or maybe a fast split?" He kicked aside an empty plastic-wrap container—one of several littering the floor. "How do you figure all these Saran Wrap boxes?"

Krug opened the half-sized refrigerator topped by an electric hot plate which constituted kitchen facilities. "Nothing in the freezer part. Beats me." He began to whistle inharmoniously, poking in the closet, examining the footlocker, tossing back the covers of the couch-bed. "Looks like fun and games here sometime lately. Maybe with the wrong cookie?" He grinned at Casey. "Don't tell me, I know. *Cherchez la femme* don't work anymore. The jealous husband bit. On the other hand—" He sighed gustily. "Come on, let's get started, sport. Whoever killed him had a reason, and maybe in this mess we can find a connection."

FIVE

"I've been hoping that wasn't really a husband you were calling," Rees said when she finally joined him at the table. "I've already ordered. Coffee and your orange juice coming right up." He hesitated. "You were a long time in that phone booth."

"Suspicious. Didn't I tell you I was calling my service? I haven't picked up any calls since yesterday afternoon."

"Miss anything important?"

"Nothing Liz Taylor won't be able to step into. You're nosy, you know that? I hate nosy people."

"Sorry. It's anxiety, I guess."

"What about?"

"You, of course."

"Oh, *heavy*," she murmured. "One of those swifty deals. So what comes next—you're lonely and misunderstood?"

Surprised at her tartness and his own reaction to it, Rees looked at her silently. Young and tough. A swinger, an actress. And the sadness that lived in him hungered for tenderness. "You didn't say, so I ordered your eggs over easy. Bacon well done. White toast."

"Groovy."

"Do you always talk like that?"

"Like what, man?"

" 'Groovy'—'heavy'—'man' every other word. I thought only the love-bead set still—"

"Oh, cool it. *Will you please cool it?*" Her eyes were suddenly liquid, luminous with tears. "I'm sorry I bug you, but I've got feelings, too. You're not the only bleeding heart—"

"Susannah, don't." He touched her hand. "I'm sorry. Really. Shall we try starting all over again?"

"Excuse *me*." The waitress set two coffees between them.

"And orange juice," Rees reminded her.

"Oops, my mistake." She beamed toothily. "Coming right up, folks." And she was gone again.

"Lawd love us, that's good," Susannah sighed after the first sip of coffee. "Staff of life. Elixir." Then mischievously she added, "Groovy," and they smiled at each other over the rims of their cups. "Despite your many failings and obvious hang-ups, I think I might like you a lot, Paul Joseph Rees."

"Likewise, I'm sure," he said happily. "Possibly the doctor might consider taking me as a patient?"

"Ve vill see, Herr Rees. Only time vill tell."

Time, he thought. Now a magic word. Suddenly he had a future.

"What's the word on our H-and-R homicide?" Krug boomed across the squad room as they walked in. "Come on, let's go. I'm not working two shifts while you assholes sit around here worrying about your sex life."

"Listen to the guy," Zwingler said, laughing, impervious as always to needling. "Like nobody else ever puts in overtime." Pudgy and rosy as a baby, he winked at his partner, Haynes. "We keep bankers' hours—right, Denny?"

But Haynes wouldn't go along with it. "Six hours OT already this week." He sniffed dolefully, a chronic sinus sufferer. "I've forgotten whether my wife's a blonde or a redhead. Al, McGregor wants you to call him soonest."

"Soonest, shit. Where the hell's his lab report?" Krug fell into his swivel chair. "Christ, I'm beat. You guys get a flyer out to the garages for collision reports?"

"Done," said Zwingler. "Car make undetermined, possible headlight damage, red paint in any scratches or dents."

"What're you talking about—red?" Then Krug blinked. "Oh, yeah, the motorcycle. Jesus, I'm so tired I'm dingy."

"Your mother just called," Haynes reported to Casey. "Said it was nothing important, she just wanted to know if you were still alive."

"Thanks, Denny." Casey kept yawning helplessly. "Right now I'm not sure it's affirmative."

"She worry about you a lot?"

"Not too much, I guess. What really bugs her is that I carry a gun. She claims it invites violence."

"Women," Haynes groaned. "So how do they expect us to nail these hoods—put salt on their tails?"

Remembering his parents' shocked faces when they had first seen him in uniform—sidearmed and sassy, fresh out of the Academy—Casey sighed. They had wanted him to be a lawyer, a professional man. Why else all that time spent acquiring an education? To them a policeman was a necessary brute, like a savage watchdog. No convincing them that the image was changing, that young men like him, the new breed, were the glue which could help keep society from disintegrating.

"Let 'em vote in some gun control laws if they're so finicky," Haynes was saying over the buzzing of incoming calls. "Maybe if they do, we'll all live longer. Listen to that phone! Hasn't stopped yet this morning...Haynes, Detective Bureau." He grimaced at the shriek coming through the receiver. "Ma'am, this *is* the Police Department, the duty man downstairs just switched your call..."

While Krug talked to the lab on an interdepartmental line, Casey used another to call the morgue downstairs. As usual, answer was slow, he had to wait through seven rings. "Decedent Barrett, G. H.," he said when a voice at the other end barked something unintelligible. "We're waiting for a prelim—"

"Prelim, my butt, we're still peeling the guy."

Casey's stomach lurched. *Peeling?*

"Listen, you want to see something wild," the voice was cackling in his ear, "come on down here and take a look. Your decedent's papered from his ass to his collarbone!"

Going down, Casey had expected another of the black humor jokes favored by the morgue assistant he'd been talking to. He gaped at the body lying on a wheeled metal table. "Oh," he said— a slow exhale which condensed in the chill air. "Papered" wasn't a joke at all, he discovered, for the corpse was wrapped in a corset fashioned from Saran Wrap. And inside the light-reflecting plastic spiraled like bandages around chest and back and belly was something greenish-colored. Blinking, Casey leaned closer.

"Yeah," said the morgue assistant. "Greenbacks, baby. Money! That's a million-dollar shroud he's wearing."

SIX

B y actual count later, the amount involved shrank to more portable proportions—fifteen hundred bills of twenty-dollar denomination. But that was later, and the magic phrase "million-dollar shroud" still burned in Casey's mind when he returned upstairs to the Detective Bureau.

"Chances're good it's a black Mercedes, all right," Krug called across the squad room when he spied Casey coming in. "They got a make on…What the hell's the matter with you?"

"Got an answer to all those empty Saran Wrap boxes."

"Who'd he deep-freeze?"

"Himself, Al." Slumping at his desk, Casey wearily explained, "So far it's all twenties. New bills. Could be counterfeit."

"You get Harry Berger on it?"

"He was out of his office, but I left a message and some samples. He'll call us as soon as he knows anything."

Leaning back, Krug fished a small cigar out of the pocket-sized cardboard box in his breast pocket. Next came a kitchen match from a side pocket. As he habitually did, he flicked it alight with his thumbnail. "Turns out to be paper, we'll have the feds on our necks." He scowled at Casey across the double expanse of their desks, which sat back to back. "Couldn't be heist money?"

"From where, for instance?"

"Uh-hunh. Okay." Krug rose, groaning. "Let's go tell our story to teacher."

At his corner desk, Lieutenant Timms listened silently, seeming to only half hear as he watched Krug's smoke rings swirling upward into the air-conditioned atmosphere. "Nice," he finally commented when Krug had finished. "This really makes my day." He surveyed them gloomily. "In the midst of all the thrills, you happen to run across anybody to identify Barrett's body? The part that isn't wrapped in money, that is?"

Krug shook his head. "All we've seen so far is a bunch of neighbors don't know nothin' about nothin'. Hoggers," he added disgustedly. "Low-life lice. So maybe the Hell's Angels're switching from dope to paper?"

"Fat chance," Timms growled. "Counterfeiting takes a brain cell or two. All right, get on the horn, see if we can get a make on this guy from R and I in LA Try Records here, too. My guess is he'll have a rap sheet as long as your arm."

But the lieutenant was wrong; there was no record for anyone named Gerald Hower Barrett at Los Angeles Police Headquarters. And local Santa Monica files were blank also.

"That's crazy," Krug fumed. "Somewhere, someplace, he's bound to have a record!"

"Well, if he has," Casey said soothingly, "Washington will let us know, Al."

"Sure, and we'll be lucky if we hear by tomorrow." Krug blew out his breath. "Okay, you goose Berger's office again while I ask teacher if we can call it a day for a while. Meet you back here like at four, okay?"

Rees noticed his suitcases first. Both were lying flat, one on top of the other. Yet he distinctly remembered sitting them on end in the corner of the motel room after he had unpacked.

The maid, he thought. She had moved the bags to vacuum the carpet. Then he noticed the faint oblong shape impressed onto the smooth bedspread. Someone had briefly rested one of his bags there. A maid wouldn't muss a bed.

Rees dived for the closet, scrabbling for the package he had hidden in the darkest corner. It was still there—a shoe box in a buff-and-black plastic bag advertising *Liljeberg's Fine Footwear, Lake Tahoe*. Lifting the box lid, he poked delicately into the toes of the brand-new handmade brogans still lying in their bed of tissue, sighing unconsciously as his fingertips encountered the lineny softness of used currency. My ill-gotten gains, he thought wryly, fishing out the roll of bills. Crapshooter's winnings. And no fault of mine some punk thief isn't set up for months with a lucky haul. Only nuts and old ladies still hide their money in their shoes.

Knowing the package wouldn't fit in his luggage, Rees had purposely left it intact, exactly as he had carried it out of the shoe store—his winner's prize. And he'd been right to do so, he thought as he admired the supple glossy leather, for the sense of luxury still lived in him, the exhilaration of exercising the mundane right of any free man with the price—to choose and buy goods without anyone's permission. These shoes were a symbol of his freedom.

The shoe box was also buff-and-black, *Liljeberg's* printed in a chic Art Nouveau style on the lid. *Lake Tahoe*. The high mountains, the tall sky had been balm for his prison-battered spirit. At night a chilly wind had soughed in the pines, and on the vast High Sierra lake, reflected stars had gleamed like submerged treasure. He had felt close to Ellen there, able to think of her again without the doomed sense of despair which had haunted him since her death. After the first day, like a soldier during truce, he had lived only in the present, enjoying everything Tahoe offered without thought of past or future.

As he slid the box back into its matching plastic bag, Rees noticed some tiny lettering in the left-hand corner of the lid. Address probably, he decided; the room was so shadowy he couldn't read it. The more expensive the store, the smaller the label always.

But when he moved into the light from the window, he saw that his guess was only half-right. The lettering spelled out only the name of the border-straddling town where impulse had taken him when he had left San Francisco: *Stateline*. His motel had been located on the California side of the imaginary line which divided the town; he hadn't realized that the shoe store, as well as the casino where he had gambled, had been located on the other side. *Stateline, Nevada.*

"Jesus," he whispered. Nevada. He'd been carrying around evidence that he had broken his parole. Only technically, of course. Unintentionally. But if someone wanted to—

Panic summoned Krug like a genie out of a bottle, and Rees could see him snooping here swiftly, disturbing nothing, missing nothing, cop face hard and blank as slate when he registered his find. Sonofabitch is careless, ain't he?—

Stop, he thought savagely. That's ex-con spook. They're not after you. Didn't Stevens warn you to watch for paranoia?

But somebody's been here, he answered himself stubbornly. And if it wasn't the maid, who the hell was it?

Trying to channel his panic, Rees methodically began checking his room. Everything in the bureau seemed the same—socks folded, shirts stacked, underwear in tidy piles. Nothing on the bureau top seemed different either. *Has* to be the maid, he reassured himself. No reason for the police to search a witness's belongings.

But if they had—he swallowed dryness. Nevada. Couldn't miss it on that box. On the list of parole conditions, leaving the state was one of the most stringent. Rees groaned aloud, slumping onto the bed as the nightmare year of imprisonment rolled over him, the suffocating despair of every day, every night. Can't, he thought. Can't go back. Better dead than sealed alive in that tomb. Then, like a voice out of the dark, he heard his parole officer's calm, even, professionally rational voice: "The worst thing you'll have to fight is the feeling that you're on the wrong side now, Paul, that we're only waiting for you to make a mistake."

Ex-con paranoia. Staring at the phone—one of many amenities advertised in neon below the Pelican Motel sign—Rees tried to blank out the terrifying vision of Krug which dominated his mind. The black plastic receiver felt slick and clammy pressed against his ear. Like a mechanical heartbeat, he heard the slow pulse of a switchboard call signal at the other end. Then the line clicked open. "Office."

"I noticed—" His voice failed and he started again. "Noticed someone's been moving my things around in here. Thought I'd better check to make sure it was one of your maids."

"Nervous, hah?" Rees recognized the twangy voice as belonging to the manager who had checked him in Friday night. "Don't blame you," he was saying cheerfully. "Saw that wad you was carrying when you paid me for your room. Better let me stow some of it in the safe here."

Rees faked a laugh. "It isn't as much as it looks." But it was, of course. Fool, he thought again. Luck had made him careless— the taste of freedom and good fortune like a bittersweet payment for all he had lost. "About the maid," he heard himself saying casually. "Didn't mean to complain, but I'd appreciate it if you'd check for me. Just if she moved my bags."

"Don't worry about a thing, Mr. Rees. But, okay, I'll check. Just enjoy yourself, hah? We got a nice place here we want everybody to enjoy. Why, folks keep coming back here from all over the country..."

Under a hot beating shower, his spirits lifted slowly, bringing a cautious optimism. Of course it was the maid. Anyone else would have been seen and surely commented upon by the gossipy manager. Paranoia, he thought again. Must watch it from now on.

Stepping out of the shower stall, Rees grabbed for one of the fluffy white towels—another advertised Pelican specialty; they were called "thirsty" on the neon sign. Water ran in his eyes, blurring the shiny bathroom, something dark-colored on the marbleized sink counter.

It was his shaving kit lying open. And something odd about it struck him as he mopped his face dry. The leather lining of the lid looked warped. No mistaking why. It had been neatly slit at one end. Just enough for an investigating hand to slide in.

Naked, chilled, Rees checked his suitcases, finding that the fabric linings in both had been slit also, top and bottom. A not very neat but thorough search. But *why?* he wondered wildly. To find his parole papers? One official call to San Francisco would have done the job in a tenth of the time it had taken to snoop here.

Sitting back on his heels, shivering, Rees savored the full bitterness of his future. Once a con always a con. Stevens was wrong. They had probably checked him immediately, he decided. Perhaps while he was still sitting there waiting to sign his name on that witness statement. And while he had breakfasted with Susannah, walked on the pier with her, driven her home…Like a cruel god, merciless and all-powerful, unforgiving, Krug loomed hugely in his mind. *Ever had any experience with the police before?* And he had lied, no. *Been out of work long?* Another lie. *You can be subpoenaed from now on…*So they had him. Like cats with a mouse. Clever cats. Stupid mouse. He was trapped in a hole of his own making.

SEVEN

"So you got yourselves a dead paperhanger, hah?" Harry Berger leaned on the counter in front of the squad room, crisply snapping one of the twenty-dollar bills which Casey had delivered to his office earlier. Officially attached to Fraud, Berger specialized in all the unviolent activities of crooks busy defrauding private citizens as well as the government—anything from kited checks to counterfeiting. "If it's the same guy," he was saying, "which I think it is, we've been looking for him since yesterday. Federal agents have been after him since last year. What's this about hit-and-run?"

"That's the story, Harry," Krug said. "And we got an eyewitness says it was murder."

"Begins to sound interesting."

Watching Berger swagger across the squad room—paunchy, balding, glossy with self-importance—Casey experienced the same guilty hope which his partner often roused in him: that he was not seeing himself in twenty years.

"Looks to me like panic time," Berger was saying. "Barrett fouls up in the dumbest way possible. Then he tries to make a break for it with a bundle before his partners find out—"

"This foul-up was a broad, maybe?"

"Right, Al. And a sixteen-year-old at that." Berger winked at Casey. "Just about right for you, hah, fella?"

"The older the cat, the younger the bird, Harry—that's a well-known sociopsychological pattern."

"Which makes Barrett what?"

"An exception to the rule, I guess."

Berger chuckled. "Okay, here's the story: we nailed this chick yesterday for passing counterfeit twenties. Bills are identical with the ones you got off Barrett's body. Our girl claims she found hers, and she's sticking to her story. But her girlfriend's not such a good liar. So far *she's* admitted that some guy picked them up Saturday night at a rock concert at Santa Monica Civic. Description sounds like your Barrett, all right. Looks like he cut our teenybopper loose from her girlfriend and balled her someplace. Probably gave her the money. Either that, or she ripped it off when he was asleep. Whichever, it's for sure he's part of a setup Treasury's been looking for since last November. All they had to go on was a phony name and a phony description. But wait a minute," he interrupted himself, "let me use your phone. I'll call the feds, see if I can set up a meeting right away. You might as well get it straight from the horse's mouth."

The meeting was scheduled for half an hour—or as soon as the Treasury agents could make it on the freeway from downtown Los Angeles. While they waited, Krug filled in the lieutenant, then silent and sour-faced he caught up on his time sheet. Knowing better than to disturb him, Casey checked downstairs in Communications to see if there was an answer yet to his query about the hit-and-run car.

There was, the clerk—an old harness bull near to retirement—informed him. "And I'll tell you something—if I didn't see it with my own eyes," the old cop said, "I wouldn't believe there could be this many people could go out and buy themselves a ten-G car." He hefted the inch-thick coded reply from Department of Motor Vehicles headquarters—a rundown on all registered owners of Mercedes automobiles in Los Angeles and satellite cities, of which Santa Monica was one. "Find the needle in the haystack. Why we could never get DMV to state color...Better forget it, young fella, you'll be a year checking out this shit."

"Anything in from Washington yet on Barrett?" Casey asked, yawning.

"Not yet. Sometimes they're slow answering. Too busy, I guess."

As Casey trudged up the stairs again, Haynes caught up with him. Denny Haynes and his partner, Ralph Zwingler, had been assigned to the shoe-leather end of the hit-and-run investigation. Casey noticed that he was limping badly.

"New shoes," Haynes explained, his voice hollow with nasal congestion. "Wore the damn things a whole month at home first. Fat lot of good it did. Anything new on Barrett?" But he didn't wait for an answer. "Been canvassing his neighborhood—you know, liquor stores, that stuff—but nobody knows from nothing about this guy. What we got was zero information."

All the outside lines were ringing when they walked into the squad room, and they both took calls. Casey's was from a nut who habitually claimed to have secret information about cases that appeared in the newspapers. This time his call concerned a suicide that had been reported in yesterday's *Evening Outlook*—really a murder, the nut declared, the decedent had been killed by relatives after her money.

Promising to check into it, Casey thanked the caller for his cooperation and hung up. The file was closed and flagged for dead records, he discovered. Information inside revealed that the decedent had been on Old Age Assistance, mortally ill, and without kin. Death had resulted from asphyxiation. Clearly the old lady had locked the door of her shabby room, turned on the gas heater, and died the lonely death of the elderly and friendless.

What a business, Casey thought. Depressed by the misery and aberration which is the policeman's unvarying climate, he stared out the second-story windows. Four hours' sleep had only made him groggy. No time to catch up, either, because they had been transferred to day tour. But with nights off again. Ah, yes, night, he thought, *nights*, and his spirits soared, expanded by visions of tomorrow evening. She'd definitely sounded eager this time. Well, maybe not exactly eager, he corrected himself realistically, but her voice over the phone this afternoon had seemed warmer, hadn't it? As if she'd been thinking about him, too?

Ms. Joanna Hill. Joey. And to think, he marveled, he'd almost missed her. Casey thought private parties were kid stuff, and he had grudgingly attended the one where he had met Joey only to keep from offending a buddy. He had spotted her immediately when he had walked in—a together-type blonde, very short pompon curly hair, big blue eyes behind granny glasses—staring unbelievingly at the buffet table loaded with delicatessen goodies and gallons of Ripple. "Time," she was saying to no one in particular, "marches backward? It's 1963 and I'm a teenybopper again." A soulmate.

She had arrived alone, too, she admitted, sandbagged like Casey by their host's insistence; he was a salesman for the firm where she worked.

"Tinytown Toys?" Delighted to have found out so quickly where to locate her, Casey blurted before he thought, "You a secretary there or something?"—a bad mistake, he knew, the instant the words were out of his mouth.

Ms. Joanna Hill was a toy designer, it turned out, and very much a professional woman. Cuddlies were her specialty, she told him after he had apologized for his male chauvinist assumption as to the nature of her work. "You know—teddy bears, bunnies—the fuzzy items."

"Then it's predestination." No response, and Casey's laughing explanation that he qualified for instant interest as a fuzzy item, too—"A cop, you dig?"—did not amuse her. Well, you win a few, you lose a few, he thought philosophically. One man's giggles, et cetera. Must watch it from now on, though. This was a serious lady…

Because he was on night tour, he had seen Joey only once since the party, a hasty hamburger lunch near her toy firm. But for the better part of two weeks since then he had fantasized about her almost continuously, his strong attraction stubbornly resisting any messages conveyed by her Lib-type cool. Definitely she's for me, he assured himself happily for the hundredth time as he stared out the second-story squad-room window. All I've got to do is convince her over dinner tomorrow—

"Okay"—Krug's harsh voice intruded on his daydream—"let's go. Time for show-and-tell on Barrett, G. H. Berger's pals from Treasury just got here."

EIGHT

"Your phone number's like riches burning a hole in my pocket. But I thought I'd get your call service. I was just dialing for practice."

"Want me to hang up so you can try again?"

Rees laughed unsteadily. "Not unless you really want to." He hesitated, savoring the syllables of her name before he spoke it. "Susannah, you sound sleepy. Sorry if I woke you."

"Always with the 'sorry.' Terrible habit." He heard her yawn. "What time is it?"

"Five after five. Susannah," he said again, urgently, "have dinner with me, will you?"

"Where, for instance?"

"Why—anyplace you say."

"Not only sorry, he's agreeable. *Agréable*," she repeated, nasally Parisian. " '*Monsieur est agréable.*' That was my first line as a dues-paying member of the acting profession."

"Sounds very convincing."

"The director didn't think so. Silly little faggot. What time?" she asked abruptly.

"Uh—six? Seven? You name it, I'll be there."

"*Agréable.* How about eight or so? We can catch the scene at the Ultimate Perception. Strictly groovy," she added, giggling. "What you might call a variation of the love-bead set."

Feeling as if he had run a race he had almost lost, Rees lay back on the bed after he had hung up, speculating on the Ultimate Perception. Restaurant? Coffeehouse? Ellen had loved the coffeehouses of San

Francisco—the real Italian places with darkly varnished interiors, huge steaming espresso machines, locals parked for hours at the tables reading newspapers with incomprehensible headlines.

Ellen. Like a slow sickness, the dreary sense of loss returned, and with it came apprehension again. The temptation that had plagued him all the time he had tried to nap came back strongly—to call Stevens in San Francisco, confess that he had lied to the police here, that he had broken his parole, and ask for help. But as he summoned the fattish pedantic face of his parole officer, Rees was certain what Stevens's answer would be: "You knew the rules, Paul, and what would happen if you broke them." That he had done so unintentionally, drunk with freedom, would not move Stevens, for he was a cop, too, wasn't he? And behind that gloss of social-worker policeman's professional compassion and understanding lived a bureaucrat blunted by dealing with misery. I'm not a man to any of them, I'm a case, Rees thought. There was no one anywhere he could really trust.

The bare-walled windowless interrogation room downstairs which Lieutenant Timms had chosen for their meeting was already thick with tobacco smoke by the time Casey and Krug entered. Seating seemed to be scarce, Casey noticed while the lieutenant briefly introduced them: the two federal agents had either taken or been given the only decent chairs, leaving a rickety metal stool meant for suspects' discomfort and a canvas folding affair which looked ready for collapse. Both bulky men, Berger and Timms had wisely passed up these, choosing instead to perch on opposite ends of the heavy, scarred oak table.

"Grab a seat," Timms told them impatiently. "We're getting caught up on background so we see what we're up against."

With a disgusted grunt, Krug hooked the metal stool closer with his foot and squatted on it near the door. Having no choice, Casey settled himself gingerly into the creaking canvas chair as the younger of the federal men briskly began the briefing.

"Two years ago, our agents in Detroit busted a petty crook named Joe Delgado. The charge was passing. That's all we could hang on him. Weren't able to crack his claim he'd bought the bundle from some character he'd never seen before. The bills he passed were twenties. Classy stuff. Printed on paper that was so close to the real thing you couldn't tell the difference. Near-perfect engraving. Reproduction that made even the experts sweat a little. All that clinched it for queer was the serial numbers—they didn't match the Treasury run. Okay! So Delgado gets sent up, and we wait for the next batch—"

"And we keep waiting," the older federal agent interrupted. "And the longer we keep waiting, the more we worry. You get a little batch of stuff this good," he explained, "nothing showing up anywhere but one spot, you know the counterfeiter's stockpiling. Usually means a bulk sale for a big discount to a syndicate, and we brace ourselves for a flood of paper across the country."

"You think Barrett was tied in with a mob?" Lieutenant Timms asked. "Mafia, maybe?"

"Not a chance. That's why he was so hard to track. No record anywhere, no connections."

"Our shadow link," his partner added. "All we knew till today was that he existed somewhere. Now at least we've got the location pinpointed." He smiled apologetically. "How about saving the questions and answers for later when I've finished?"

Flushing slightly, Timms nodded.

"Okay," the young Treasury man went on, "it's watch-and-wait time after we nail Delgado. We know somebody's got the plates and equipment. The question is, Why isn't he—or they—printing any more of this nearly foolproof paper?"

The answer, he said, came six months later when Delgado made a break from the prison farm where he had been sent after a period of good behavior in a federal cellblock. Knowing he'd probably had help in the break, authorities watched his family and known friends, particularly a woman he'd been seeing before he was sent up. Nothing happened for a week—Delgado was hiding out obviously—then suddenly his girlfriend turned up missing.

"*Cherchez la femme*," Krug muttered, grinning at Casey. "See, it still works."

Both federal agents smiled, but it was obvious that the younger one resented the interruption. "Delgado's girlfriend delivered a car and some money to him," he continued in a slightly louder tone. "Pretty clever about it, too. Delgado would have been long gone if he hadn't piled up in a rainstorm and panicked. His leaving the wreck got the local police interested, and they traced the car back to his girlfriend. Meanwhile Delgado kept stealing cars, driving a hundred miles or so, then abandoning them. Left a trail so clear even a blind man could have followed it. We traced him to a town in Kentucky, just across the Ohio border. Asked for cooperation from the local police, of course. What we wanted them to do was keep their eyes open, and when they spotted Delgado, to leave him to us. But instead some eager beaver dropped on him."

"These local cops." Timms shook his head mournfully. "On TV they always foul up, too."

"No offense intended, Lieutenant," the older agent said soothingly. "All we're trying to do is fill you in." He nodded to the other one to go on.

As usual, his partner continued, Delgado refused to talk, and he was extradited from Kentucky to stand trial for additional sentencing. Meanwhile, working on the assumption that Delgado might have been headed for the counterfeiter for a second crack at the big score he had missed the first time, Treasury agents in Kentucky canvassed the border town and the surrounding countryside searching for the counterfeiting plant. "Finally found it in an old barn out in the country," he said ruefully. "What was left of it, that is. A small press, and a pile of waste they hadn't even bothered to bum. No mistaking it was the place we were looking for. But all the valuable stuff was gone, naturally. Plates, cameras, photo-processing equipment. We knew they could set up again anywhere they could find an offset press."

"Where does Barrett fit in?" Timms asked impatiently.

"That we're not sure of, Lieutenant. Either he was part of the original operation, or he came in later when they relocated."

"Kansas," the senior agent said. "Just outside Lawrence. But by the time we caught up with them—it was a family, incidentally—our master counterfeiter was dying of cancer, and the equipment had disappeared. This was months later. And with everything gone, no evidence, our hands were tied. We figured the wife had sold out, but there wasn't any way of proving it."

"But we had one thread left," his partner added. "A guy one of the daughters had been seen with. The name he used was Howe. Jerry Howe. A floater, according to the local police. Lived in a rooming house, no bank accounts, no voter registration, no past or future we could catch up with."

"Barrett," Casey said.

"That's a pretty good guess."

"Not so good," Harry Berger corrected him irritably. "I already told 'em Barrett was probably our man."

" 'A phony name,' " Casey quoted, " 'and a phony description.' Has to be the one the family sold out to. Why else would they try to protect him?"

"Wait a minute," the younger agent said, "you're missing some parts. Don't forget a lot of time has elapsed in this story. What we figure is, they planned a big sale of paper to a Detroit syndicate, and Delgado was to arrange it. The paper he had was sample stuff to show the quality."

"A crook is a crook," Timms sighed. "Couldn't resist the temptation to spend some, right?"

"Something like that. We think it scared our counterfeiters when they heard he'd been busted. They were amateurs, don't forget. And by this time, their technician was probably good and sick. Anyway, when Delgado showed up again, they panicked and took off."

" 'Last chance in Kansas,' " Krug said. "The dying counterfeiter. Sounds like soap opera stuff."

"Yeah, it is in a way," the senior federal man agreed. "We had an agent sitting in the hospital while the guy was dying. Took him three months. Poor bastard wouldn't admit anything—didn't want to incriminate his family, of course. Kept saying all he wanted was to leave them some money. It was an obsession with him. We think he'd known for three years or more he had cancer. And he was a master engraver—what else was he going to think up to make a fast fortune? The only thing he forgot was he'd have to deal with crooks after he'd done his own work."

"About Barrett," Timms reminded him.

"Yes. Well. What we think is, he wanted in, but by this time, the family was finished with Daddy's big scheme. But Barrett— or Howe, as he called himself then—wouldn't let it go."

"Should've married the daughter," Krug grunted. Then he peered at the older agent. "Or did he?"

"Nothing on record we know of, Sergeant. On the other hand," he added, "he did all right for himself. Managed to persuade them to give him a chance to buy the stuff. We were pretty sure of that because the day after the father was hospitalized for the last time, Howe disappeared. Went looking for financing obviously."

"And you think he found it here?" Timms asked.

"Got to be, Lieutenant. He made his connections, and before the month was up he was back in Kansas. According to neighbors there, a U-Haul truck moved some stuff out of the house the family had rented. Out of the basement, they claimed. And all of a sudden, there was money for the hospital bills the family claimed they couldn't pay two days earlier." He spread his hands. "Figures, doesn't it? They sold out to Barrett. He brought the stuff here. Since last December, he's been busy setting up and manufacturing."

"Probably the same deal," the younger agent said gloomily. "One huge shipment discounted to a syndicate. We'll get hit with a blizzard of phony twenties some mob paid ten cents on the dollar for."

The Treasury agents left shortly afterward, followed by Lieutenant Timms. But Berger and Krug and Casey lingered on in the interrogation room, sipping coffee out of the vending machine which Krug, playing host, paid for. "From paperhanging to murder—that's a pretty big jump, Harry." Krug blew steam off his paper cup of sweetened brew. "And a hit like that, figures they got to be amateurs."

Berger nodded. "Panic time, like I said. Now all we got to look for is a nervous printer, right? Which means one out of about a million people. Every other block has a so-and-so press in the west district. I'm not even thinking beyond that. Christ, we'll be till Doomsday checking 'em out!"

"Don't forget your pigeons've got fair warning, too," Krug added. "Could be they'll make a hurry-up deal."

"I know." Berger looked despondent. "On the other hand, we could have a slight edge, too." His sudden smile was ferocious. "After all, you've got that eyewitness. Some nice juicy bait. Maybe all we have to do is wait and see who comes pecking around him."

"But we can't do that," Casey protested. "If anything, we should provide Rees with protection."

Krug snorted. "You want to hear the biggest sob story in town, try that one on Timms."

He wasn't wrong, Casey found when he did.

"Sure, we can even hold him as a material witness," the lieutenant agreed wearily. "So along comes his lawyer, screaming harassment of the innocents, and then what?" He was silent for a moment, studying the duty roster. "Can't put a round-the-clock watch on him either. We're strained to the limit as it is. Most we might do is a man at night. But even if anything happens, he'd have to watch out for himself daytimes."

"Then shouldn't he be warned, sir?"

"We risk losing him if we do." Timms shook his head. "No, the best we can do for now is keep his name out of the papers. Keep track of him as best we can, see what happens. Chances are, if it doesn't look too dangerous, they'll lie low. The last thing they'll fall for is any bait idea."

Krug grinned when Casey reported the conversation. "Better hope he's right, hah?" He laughed at Casey's expression. "Let's get a query on Rees off to Frisco anyhow. The least we can do is find out who and what he is, now that Mr. Clean might be changing his name to Unlucky."

NINE

The answer to their query to Washington Central Bureau was a disappointment—a terse statement attesting to the happy anonymity still enjoyed by citizens who manage to avoid entanglement with the law or subversive organizations. But their request for information regarding possible military service by the decedent was more rewarding. Gerald Hower Barrett had been inducted into the Army in 1968 from North Platte, Nebraska. As next of kin he had listed a mother, Mrs. Ada Taylor Barrett, also of North Platte, to whom he had assigned an allotment. No medals and one promotion signaled a mediocre soldier. Barrett had seen brief service in Vietnam. In 1972 he had received an honorable discharge.

Timms put in a long-distance call to the chief of police of North Platte, talking only briefly. "Watch the teletype," he said when he hung up. "Seems they pride themselves on fast coopera-tion with other forces."

Krug snorted. "Don't hold your breath. I've waited for these prairie dudes to get out of their gopher holes before."

But North Platte answered in less than half an hour. "I don't believe this," Timms marveled. "It's really the word! His mother's an invalid. Hasn't seen Barrett since he was shipped overseas. Looks like he's kept in fairly close touch, though. Postcards, Christmas cards, an occasional letter."

"So what do we do," Krug demanded, "about getting him identified?"

"Don't give up, Al. There's a sister, it says here. They're going to try to track her down right away. They'll let us know how they make out in an hour or so." Timms leaned back in his swivel chair, groaning softly, rubbing the nape of his neck. "So that's that for now. Looks like all we've got in the way of a solid lead is that teenybopper. The one who was passing the phony twenties."

"Name, Maryanna Hawkins," the Juvenile man, Abner Lilly, read off from his case file. "Called Yanna by her friends and family. She's a student at Samohi. Pretty good grades, no trouble before. But that may change now," he predicted moodily. "Nobody but Mommy and Daddy bought her story about finding the counterfeit money, but she stuck to it, so what could we do? Score one for her. We gave her the usual warning, and released her to her parents."

"Hope they tanned her butt for her." Krug growled.

"You're kidding—in this age of the sacred child? They're probably both at the nearest shrink right now, trying to find out how they failed their little darling."

"What's her girlfriend's name?" Casey inquired. "The one she went to the rock concert with?"

"Elise Janoff."

"You talk to her at all?"

"Not enough to get a real line on her," Lilly admitted. "Shy type—or playing it that way. The Hawkins girl is obviously the dominant partner. But if you could scare the other one a little, work on her guilt, you might get something out of her."

"How about these Hawkinses," Krug asked while Casey took down the addresses for both girls. "They nice-type people? Respectable citizens?"

"Sure." Lilly shrugged. "Only the kid's got 'em buffaloed. You know the story. Sixteen years old, she knows all the answers, they got nothing to give her but the Establishment line."

"Another teenybopper philosopher." Krug grunted. "Okay, we get 'em every day, Ab, no sweat."

"That's what you think," was Lilly's parting shot. "After I got through with Yanna-baby, *I* felt like I'd been in a steambath!"

The Hawkins house was in a quiet neighborhood not too far from where Casey lived. Two blocks away was Lincoln Junior High, but Santa Monica High School was miles to the south. She probably rode her bike there as he had, Casey guessed. Or caught a bus. Only the tenderer types were chauffeured by mothers made anxious by accident and crime statistics.

"Nice hydrangeas," Krug commented as they trudged up the walk, squinting in the late, low sun hanging over the distant invisible sea. "Mine've got some kind of infestation. Keep spraying 'em every week, but the damn bugs seem to like the stuff. Next thing I know they'll be spitting it back at me."

Casey punched the doorbell and they listened to chimes inside.

"Yes?" a voice called after a moment from somewhere. "I'm over here." A pleasant-looking woman in her late thirties was peering around the corner of the building—a gardener, they saw; Yanna's mother, she told them. "Oh, no," she moaned when they identified themselves. "Not police again—"

"No problem, Mrs. Hawkins," Casey told her hastily. "We only want to talk to her for a minute."

"Well, she's doing her homework now. At least, I hope she is. They're so independent, aren't they? I was never that independent Why, when *my* parents—Oh, never mind. This way." She started down the driveway, pulling off her gardening gloves. "Excuse the back door, but the front's locked. My husband always insists on it when he's not home."

The kitchen was shiny-clean, Casey noticed as they followed her in, remodeled several years ago probably, color-schemed to match the bronzy appliances. Through an open door, he glimpsed a wide hall which had been made into a picture gallery. Prosperous, trendy, culture-hip, middle-class, the Hawkinses would be knowledgeable about wines, he guessed, music, the theater—everything, in fact, but their daughter.

"Darling." Mrs. Hawkins was tapping timidly on a door to what had been meant to serve as a maid's quarters. From within came a squalling voice over pounding rock rhythm—the late Janis Joplin, Casey recognized. "Darling? Yanna?"

"What *is* it?" a young voice called bitchily, and Krug glanced at Casey. Uh-hunh.

"There're some men here to see you, dear. Policemen."

Something banged inside. Then the music cut off. A second later, the door opened revealing a short girl with a huge mop of fuzzy golden hair.

"Just a couple questions, Yanna," Krug said, smoothly stepping around the mother. "Mind if we come in?" And once they were in, he smiled at Mrs. Hawkins, blocking her way in. "Only be a minute, ma'am." He closed the door in her face.

"So what's the hassle?" Blue eyes shining, face pink, the girl glared at them. But it was halfway an act, Casey decided. Behind the sexpot stance—legs apart, hands on hips—something could be sensed that was still tender and capable of alarm.

"Just take it easy, Yanna," Krug was saying. "Nothing to be scared of."

"Who said I was scared, pig?"

Ignoring her, Krug glanced around the room—a little study, apparently, with bookshelves, posters on the walls, a huge office desk taking up most of the floor space. "Nice," he commented. "This your dad's den?"

"What's it to you?"

"Nothing." He smiled placidly. "How about if we sit down for a minute?"

"I've got homework to do."

"Yeah, your mother told us. Time for finals, hah?" Krug twiddled with the dials on the small transistor radio sitting on the desk. "You always study with the music going?"

"When I feel like it. Hey, man," she protested as Krug seated himself at the desk, "*I was sitting there!*"

Krug grinned, settling himself comfortably.

"Shit," she muttered. "*Fuckin' fuzz.*" She dropped into a shabby armchair, curling her blue-jeaned legs under her—a sweet-sour dumpling, Casey thought as he chose a straight chair near the door.

On the other side of the panel, he could hear the floor squeaking. Mrs. Hawkins was eavesdropping. The missing Mr. Hawkins was due for an earful.

"Barrett," Krug was saying. "Gerald Hower Barrett." He hesitated, staring at the girl until she began to fidget. "You read about him in the *Outlook* this afternoon maybe? No? Sure?" He made a disapproving tch-tch sound. "Ought to read your local paper, keep up with what's going on. Or maybe you didn't even know your shack-up's name?"

The girl kept licking her lips—a nervous tic, Casey realized, but it looked enticing, lascivious. Her voice, when it came out at last, was too shrill, defensive: "What're you talking about, pig? I don't know anybody—"

"He's dead, Yanna. Somebody killed him." Krug leaned toward the girl, his voice lowered clandestinely. "Let's start at the beginning, okay? At that rock concert. And never mind what you told your folks, we want the truth, understand? Chapter and verse, Yanna. He picked you up at Santa Monica Civic—and then what?"

TEN

"If I had any kids," he was fuming half an hour later, "I'd poison 'em, do the world a favor. Turn right here."

"It's left, Al." Casey made a screeching turn through the yellow warning signal, barely missing a car that had rushed the opposite traffic light.

"Jesus!" Krug braked unconsciously in the passenger seat. One of these days, Casey knew, the floorboards would go through. "Anybody ever tell you you're a menace on the road?"

"Not in the last hour. Al, we're not going to get anyplace trying to bully these kids."

"Bullshit. Pushing 'em is the *only* way we'll nail 'em." Raising his voice in a poor falsetto imitation of a girl's, he said, " 'Man, we rapped with a lot of dudes. Practically everybody at Civic Saturday night!' Who's she think she's kidding?"

"Us, and so far she's doing fine, I'd say."

"Yeah, well, we'll see about that when we hit her girlfriend."

Glimpsing his partner's angry, fiery face from the corner of his eye, Casey smiled to himself, recalling Abner Lilly's comment that his session with Yanna had left him feeling like he'd been in a steambath. Krug looked as if he'd spent the week in one.

"Don't like witnesses who lie," he was saying savagely. "And for damn sure I don't like sassy little bitches making a fool out of me!"

"I dig, Al. All I'm suggesting is we try another line."

"Like what, for instance?" Casey explained his idea, but Krug only grunted. But as they pulled up in front of the apartment building where Elise Janoff lived, he said grudgingly, "Okay, try it your way. But if it don't work, I'm hauling both of 'em in. Maybe a night or two getting chased around by some baby dyke at Juvenile might straighten 'em out."

Elise would be back in perhaps ten minutes, the thin tiny old lady who opened the door of the Janoff apartment informed them. Would the gentlemen care to wait?

Surprised at her lack of curiosity as to who they might be, Casey identified himself properly and said if she didn't mind, yes, they'd like to wait. "This is my partner, Detective Sergeant Krug."

"So," she murmured. "Policemen. Well, come in, please." She showed them into a living room crammed with dark, heavy Old World furniture.

"You're a member of Elise's family, ma'am?" Casey inquired.

"Grandmother, yes." Her heavy-lidded, weary eyes closed briefly. "Poor child, I am her only family. Imagine. So young and only an old foreigner to talk with. We are like creatures, I think, from two distant planets. But excuse me," she went on briskly. "I have not said my name, or asked you to sit. I am Elisaveta Janoff. Her father's mother. May he rest in peace." She shook hands delicately, using her fingertips only, then gestured toward two massively carved thronelike chairs sitting by the large front window. "Please be comfortable. You will take refreshment?"

"No thanks, ma'am," Krug replied before Casey could. "We'll just wait here if you've got something else to do."

The idea seemed to astonish Elisaveta Janoff, and she smiled uncertainly, obviously at a loss as to how to answer. "I bring tea," she declared finally, and excusing herself, left the room.

" 'Two distant planets,' " Krug muttered when an inner door had closed behind her. "She hit it on the button, all right. How d'you figure a kid like that other one fitting in here?"

"Beyond me, Al." Casey glanced around, savoring the atmosphere of another world. "Looks like a museum."

"*Mausol*eum, you mean." Krug grinned at his own cleverness. "You want to change your mind about handling the questions and answers?"

Casey was about to say no when the front door opened. They glimpsed a young female hand on the knob, heard a light clear voice crooning something, then a small dog like an animated ragheap trotted in and began barking shrilly.

"Stop it—Oh!" Poised in the doorway, the small, dark, cleverlooking girl stared in at them—surprised at first, Casey saw, then shocked, then frightened. But by the time she had closed the door, she had recovered herself.

"You're Elise Janoff, miss?" he inquired. "We're police officers." They both flashed their identifications. "We'd like to ask you a few questions."

The dog kept growling at them, and she snatched it up, hugging it to her. "Stop it, Pupsi." Casey saw her swallowing nervously. "I suppose—suppose you've been talking to my grandmother?"

"Not yet," said Krug, coming down hard on the last word. "And if you're a smart girl, Elise, maybe we won't have to."

Oh, great, Casey thought disgustedly. So after an opening punch like that I'm supposed to carry on with the friendly local fuzz bit? Trying to allay the girl's nervousness, he began with a series of mild questions about her activities at Samohi, hobbies if any, friends both male and female in and out of high school. She didn't make the mistake of leaving Yanna Hawkins off the list, and when Casey let the name go by without comment, she seemed encouraged enough to chatter a bit, mostly about her flute playing and the possibility of a musical career later. Mozart was her favorite composer, she admitted.

"Classical bag," Casey commented to Krug. "No rock, no jive, no down home blues."

Elise giggled nervously, and they both looked at her, waiting. "We-ell," she drawled, obviously imitating someone, "that's a heavy scene, yeh, but it's not all of it, man. There's room for everybody."

"Like the Stones?" Casey suggested, and she nodded. Yes, the Rolling Stones were fine. "Like the Grateful Dead? Like—?" He kept naming rock groups, at last dropping the one that had played Saturday night at Santa Monica Civic Auditorium. "Your friend Yanna likes them, too. She told us you stayed through four encores, and whooped it up for more till they finally had to turn out the lights."

"Yes, it was a good concert." She was stiff now, abruptly reverting to Grandmother's girl. "We enjoyed it very much."

"No, you didn't," Casey said gently. "And you're a lousy liar, Elise. Better give up trying."

Her eyes darted toward the inner door her grandmother had gone through. "What—what do you mean?"

"The man who picked up your girlfriend at the concert was murdered early this morning."

The girl's mouth opened, but nothing came out.

"His name was Gerald Barrett, and we're sure his death has some connection with that money Yanna got from him."

"Don't tell my grandmother," she whispered. "*Please* don't! She wouldn't understand, you see. From the old country, and she—she—"

Her voice broke suddenly and she began to cry in a quiet, hopeless, despairing way which tore at Casey. Despising himself, his rotten bullying job, he gritted his teeth. Without looking at Krug, he said, "Elise, we're not here to torment you. Or Yanna either. But we've got to know the truth. You can't protect her anymore, it's gone beyond that now."

By the time they checked into the squad room again, it had been dark for what seemed hours to Casey. Another report was in from North Platte PD, they discovered. Barrett's sister had been located and notified of her brother's death. "According to the chief, she's taking a bus to someplace called Grand Island," Timms told them. "From there she'll catch the first plane west, so for sure she'll be here tomorrow. Any luck with the kid?"

"Kids, you mean," Krug corrected him sourly. "If it wasn't for the girlfriend, we'd be up shit creek for sure. You tell it," he added wearily to Casey. "I'm too beat to try to sort out all that teenybopper guff."

Baloney, Casey thought. The guff was already sorted, checked where possible, question-marked where not. They had left both Yanna and her mother in tears. "Barrett buzzed them during the intermission," he began. "Big dude making the scene. You know the type, sir. A few joints he's willing to share, a few bucks or something to the guy in the seat next to them so he can move in and take over. By the end of the concert Yanna was stoned out of her mind and ready for anything."

"So they ditch the girlfriend?"

Casey nodded. "Yanna was supposed to spend the night at Elise's, so she didn't even have to think of a story to call home. She and Barrett split during the encores. Elise went home alone, of course. Grandma was asleep, so no problem there. But I guess she worried all night anyway."

"Good thing she did," Krug commented. "Made it easy for Yanna to lie so she could swear to it."

"About five the next morning—that's Sunday," Casey went on, "Elise said she came tapping on the door."

"Ready to tell all to her square little friend, I suppose." Timms grimaced. He had daughters of his own—but grown, naturally. "Girls will be girls. Okay, what next?"

"We took the story back to Yanna."

Timms peered at him suddenly. "She a pretty girl? Maybe old for her age?"

Casey could feel himself flushing. "Yes, sir, I'd say she was."

"Glands," Krug muttered. "And boy, has she got 'em! That kid's as hot—"

"All right, Al, don't blow a gasket, I get the picture." Timms nodded to Casey. "Go on, I'm listening."

"We hit her with Elise's story, but she denied everything at first, and bad-mouthed Elise some." He glanced at Krug. "So we told her we'd have to take her in."

"Not kosher." Timms grinned. "But okay—then what?"

"She didn't break till we invited Mama in to listen." Casey sighed unconsciously. "They both had hysterics, then Mama called Daddy long distance and told him."

"Guy had balls enough to listen anyway," Krug added. "At a buck or so a minute, I gave it to him the second time straight, no holds barred. Then he asked me to put the kid on. Took her about two minutes after Daddy got through with her to wrap it up for us." He glanced at Casey. "Your move again, sport."

"Well, there isn't much more." Casey consulted his notebook. "She kept saying she was too stoned to remember much. Seems he was driving a car—she doesn't know what kind—and they didn't go directly to his pad. She was a little confused about the details, but what it sounded like, he'd either borrowed the car or jumped it. Anyway, they drove down some alley to a garage, she remembers. A ratty old place, she said, maybe around Fifth or Sixth. She thinks Colorado was the nearest cross street."

"This a public garage she meant?"

"No, sir, sounded to me like it belonged to a house. And there was a motorcycle in the garage, she said. Barrett wheeled that out, then put the car in. They went the rest of the way to his pad on the cycle."

Timms leaned back in his chair, staring at the ceiling, appearing to digest the story. "Fifth or Sixth near Colorado," he muttered. "Probably one of those old houses that backs up to the alleys. You're sure she said the garage opened into the alley?"

"That's what she said, sir."

"Could be one he rented from a private party. Worth a fast look, anyway, see if we get lucky for a change." The lieutenant glanced at his watch. "Not too late to try either. You two got pep enough left for a last push?"

It took them slightly over an hour of ringing doorbells to find the place—an old shingle-sided bungalow half buried under a tangle of bougainvillaea which hadn't been trimmed in years. Under his middle name, Hower, Barrett had rented their garage for ten dollars a month, the old couple who owned the house told them. One of those bearded young ones, the wife added, but nice enough. No trouble at all, her husband agreed. Hower had paid on the dot every month regularly since last December.

Krug asked if they had a duplicate key and they admitted they had. But the old man refused to turn it over to them. "Him paying me like that kinda makes it his, don't it?" he demanded. "Like an apartment or a house you rent? So that means you fellas got to give me some kinda court order to get in."

"It's the goddam TV," Krug groused when they had finally persuaded the old people, and, key in hand, plodded through the weed-grown backyard revealed by the flashlight which Casey carried as standard equipment. "They're all lawyers after watching sixteen reruns of Perry Mason. Give you an argument every time you so much as punch their doorbell."

The gate which let into the alley looked ready to fall down, one hinge off, the other so frozen by corrosion that they had to force it. The alley was deserted at this hour, eerily quiet, and unconsciously they lowered their voices. Krug held the flashlight while Casey tried the key in the cheap padlock fastening the weatherbeaten double doors of the garage. The key worked easily. Grunting, Krug heaved the left door open while Casey struggled with the right one. Then silently they stared in at the glossy car which the flashlight revealed. A black sedan. Unmistakably a Mercedes-Benz.

"Glory hallelujah," Krug breathed. "Could we *be* this lucky?" The car was a tight fit in the garage, and trying to squeeze by to get a look at the front, he got stuck on a nail. "Here, goddam-mit!" He tossed the flashlight to Casey. "Crawl over the top if you have to!"

But Casey was able to slide by on the other side. "Eureka," he said softly. "One broken headlight. Red paint on the bumper—"

"Okay, stand by while I call the garage." There was an ugly ripping sound, and Krug cursed furiously. "I'm gonna sue the goddam city one of these days, all the pants I've wrecked—"

Listening to the back gate slam, Krug's number elevens plowing through the weeds, Casey leaned on the hood of the Mercedes, laughing helplessly. Who would have believed that Detective Sergeant Krug would wear tiger-striped peekaboo nylon underwear? Good old Uncle Al, no end to his marvels.

The tow truck from the police garage arrived ten minutes later. "Hands off the inside," Krug instructed. "Nobody but Fingerprint gets the first look, right?"

"Anything you say," the driver agreed, grinning. "Love your shorts, sweetie. Bet the wifie really gets turned on—"

"Shut up, asshole. And lock up that garage when you're finished."

"Sure thing, Tiger."

Casey burned rubber getting back to the station, but for once Krug had no complaints about their speed. Fatigue for-gotten now, they got a temporary release of the keys found on Barrett's body from Property. Next they went to the lab, where they were in luck again, for McGregor wasn't busy. Without delay, he assured them, he and his technicians would go to work on the Mercedes.

"Last stop," Krug puffed as they climbed the stairs once more. "You start the reports. I'll call Timms at home—"

But the lieutenant was still at his corner desk. "Got news for you," he called when they walked into the squad room. "Looks like your hunch about Rees was right, Al. Take a look at this."

"A record?" Krug scanned the rap sheet. "Served one year of a three-year sentence. Jesus Christ, for felony manslaughter! Released to San Francisco Parole Authority last month—"

"Too late to call them now," Timms said. "But we'll want to get hold of them first thing tomorrow. Could be they're looking for the guy."

"Better believe it," Krug said grimly. "That lying son of a bitch, not one damn thing he told us is the truth. So maybe that goes for his story about just happening to see a homicide, too?" Then he rounded on Casey furiously. "And *you* been worrying about protecting him. Christ, for all we know he could be the fingerman for that bunch of murdering paperhangers!"

ELEVEN

In more ways than he had imagined, the Ultimate Perception turned out to be a surprise for Rees. First, it was a seaside place—which Susannah hadn't mentioned—and, second, it catered to the sort of clientele that made her description of it as "a variation of the love-bead set" maliciously inexact.

A graveled parking lot almost filled with cars separated the two-storied wooden structure built on pilings from the Coast Highway. Counting the Cadillacs, Jags and a pair of Rolls-Royces as they crossed the lot, Rees decided he was in for a very expensive evening. Well, Malibu, he thought, sniffing the chill, salty sea air, you pay for scenery anywhere in the world. Like Sausalito, this was gilt-edged country. He was glad that at least his new shoes might measure up to the level of affluence inside. Certainly from head to toe, Susannah would.

"You look marvelous," he told her as he opened the door of the restaurant. "I feel like a male Cinderella out with the Mod Princess."

"Well, thank you, Cindy." she giggled. "Just don't turn into a pumpkin when you meet your wicked old sisters."

Following her into the plush music-filled dusk of a tiny open foyer, Rees glimpsed huge windows across the bar lounge to the right, a breathtaking floodlit view of barnacled rocks, tide pools, a surging comber about to break with a roar. To the left was a long dining area and a panorama of Santa Monica Bay. All the tables were occupied, as were all the bar stools, and as his eyesight adjusted, Rees realized what Susannah had meant by her enigmatic remark: the customers were all men.

"You like?" she asked teasingly.

"Ask me in Pumpkin."

"Oh, right *on*, man!" Her laughter was a shout. "As a matter of fact," she subsided, giggling again, "the food is great here."

"Well, if I can pass when the glass slipper starts making the rounds—"

A slender long-haired type in skin-tight yellow suede trousers and a striped shirt of neon hues bustled up to them carrying an armful of large elaborate menus. "Sorry, no deuces for at least—Oh, it's you," he said to Susannah. "For one mad moment I thought Suburbia had invaded us."

"It has, sweetie, but don't worry about it," she said tartly. "We'll just sup, and slum, and slither out quietly before the witching hour. Paul, this is Freddy. Freddy, Paul. Don't do that," she warned as Rees extended his hand. "It's called groping here."

"Bitch," Freddy murmured. He shook Rees's hand as if the gesture was strange to him. "All right, get yourselves a drink, sweeties. I'll have a table for you in ten minutes."

"You get a drink, Paul," Susannah said. "I'll go commune with my image a little bit."

Feeling deserted, Rees located a space at the crowded bar and ordered himself a martini. While he waited for it to arrive he watched the waves lifting and crashing against the rocks outside, trying to ignore the heavily sibilant conversations around him. One end of the bar seemed to be a gathering spot for muscle boys in sleeveless tank tops and paper-thin jeans—a club within a club, Rees decided when he noticed that that section of the back bar was dominated by an elaborately framed life-sized photo study of a nearly nude Mr. America type. The proprietor, perhaps? Ultimate Perception, Rees thought wryly, studying the ridiculous muscleman pose. Meaning narcissism.

The martini was excellent, he discovered, and after the first couple of sips, he decided not to be annoyed with Susannah for bringing him here. After all, an actress, he thought. Show business was notoriously full of homosexuals. It probably meant nothing to her. Less uneasy, since he was being completely ignored by the nearby customers, he turned with his drink to watch for her.

But when Susannah appeared, it wasn't out of the door marked *Powder Room* as he'd expected. Instead, she ran lightly down the stairway clearly labeled *Private*, and at the bottom, turned to speak to someone on the stairs whom Rees could not see. More telephoning? he wondered. This time he wouldn't make the mistake of asking. As she started toward the bar obviously looking for him, he beckoned, but to his surprise she walked right by him. Irritated and suspicious of some feminine game, Rees watched her until he realized that she was really searching for him. My God, he thought, she must be blind as a bat. "Susannah?" His heart turned over as she whirled, smiling.

"—And one of these days I'm going to invent a talking menu, too," she said, finishing her astonishing tirade against eyeglasses when they were finally settled at a table by the window. "All the oculists'll fight me, but I'll make a million anyway. Bifocals will be a thing of the past."

So she was near-sighted, too. "Be interesting to see what happens on the highways," Rees commented dryly. "A million fatalities a year maybe? No more problems about overpopulation."

"See, it all works out according to Roche's Law. 'What you can't see'—"

" 'Can only kill you'?" Laughing with her, Rees was conscious of a subtle shift inside himself which made his delight in her false. What you can't see. Headlights flared in his mind, then abruptly went out. He heard the soft solid thump of the impact— "My God," he breathed, "you couldn't even see that car this morning! Why didn't you tell the police—?"

"I *did* see it! A blur anyway. A green—Oh, forget it, I don't want to talk about it."

"But you should have explained—"

"*I said I don't want to talk about it.*" Their silence was like a vacuum instantly filled by the voices around them. Susannah turned to look out the window, her reflection on the dark pane remote, utterly withdrawn. "What a downer," she said so softly he scarcely heard. "You're one of those spoilers, aren't you? Knew it when we were having breakfast. Man, did I know it! The Dude Who Kills Giggles—"

"Susannah, don't. I'm sorry."

"You're always sorry."

The waiter came by, and he ordered two double martinis in hopes that alcohol might mend the evening. And it did, but only partially: through more drinks and a winy dinner, he was sadly aware that she was performing for him rather than enjoying his company. Spoiler, he kept thinking. The Dude Who Kills—

"But think of the vitamins," she was saying. "Stone-ground whole wheat. Organically grown veggies. Who cares about steak and baked potato?"

Dizzily recalling that their latest subject was vegetarianism versus the sort of cholesterol-laden food they had just enjoyed, Rees made himself smile. "Even full, the beast inside howls red meat when it hears the word 'vegetarian.' Man is, after all, a carnivore."

"Getting off on words." She made a face. "So how about the Chinese? How about the Hindus, man? The whole Third World is practically meatless."

"That's poverty, not conviction."

"Oh, man, you are impossible. Vot does a Doktor do vit a patient like this?"

Comfort me with apples. Heal me with honey. And all the days of my life, Ellen's voice echoed softly in him. *All the days—*

"How about a brandy? Waiter, two Hennesseys here." It was a

long time since he had known the shallow, bittersweet surcease of drunkenness.

His head felt like a melon split in two parts by the time they left the restaurant—some sensitive heretofore-hidden core of consciousness exposed now, pithy and overripe. Aware of her scent, warmth which made the sensitized skin of his hands and face tingle, Rees glared straight ahead, driving extra carefully. From the corner of his eye, he could see her beside him, feel her breathing, sense her pulse. Desire, the appetite that feeds upon itself. And in this case, he thought, so uselessly. "How about another brandy someplace?"

"*Such* a thirsty dude." He saw that she was smiling. "You keep this up, you'll be wiped out before we get there. But Jervis boozes like it's going out of style tomorrow, too."

"I've missed something. Who's Jervis?"

"The party, man." She shifted in the seat, facing him. "Oh God," she sighed after a moment. "Forgot to tell you. We're supposed to go on to this bash. But we don't have to if you don't want to."

But we do, of course, because she called from the restaurant to say we would. Or did she? Confused, he vaguely remembered seeing the public phone in the restaurant located in the foyer by the restrooms—

The party was back in Santa Monica, Susannah was saying, literally only a stone's throw from their own places on Ocean Avenue. A long stone's throw, he discovered, for the house sat on the beachfront hundreds of feet below the palisades which Ocean Avenue skirted. Rees guessed it might be one of the long line of palatial-looking residences he had admired yesterday when he had walked in the narrow park at the top of the bluffs. From his bird's-eye view, he had seen precious-looking pools and gardens, all shut off from the public beach by high walls and shrubbery.

But the house they finally stopped at was south of these, one of a cluster of weatherbeaten frame cottages just north of the pier.

From the curbside they could hear the din of the party, and as Susannah opened the door without bothering to knock, a female voice shrieked clearly, "Ooo-wow-you-*scare*-me!"

Well, at least it's on the straight side here, Rees thought gloomily. Maybe.

Ooo-wow-you-scare-me. He was to hear the same five words screamed with exactly the same emphasis like a running refrain for the rest of the evening. "That's her thing," Susannah explained one of the few times he was able to locate her in the crush of guests. "She's not programmed for anything else this year." Then she disappeared again.

Feeling like a foreigner, ignorant of custom, language, any mode of communication save smiles, Rees wandered around with a drink in his hand, watching blue-jeaned unisex dancers gyrating to deafening rock records. Other groups dressed in poor-boy overalls or High Tack finery clustered together, rapping and puffing joints. Fragments of conversations and glimpses of faces over shoulders wheeled like confetti in the electronic downpour which assailed Rees's senses. He kept trying to locate Jervis, kept looking for Susannah, finding neither. That he didn't even know what his host looked like seemed some final negative triumph of alienation.

The entire house had been given over to the party, he discovered as he drifted slowly from room to room, beginning to enjoy his Invisible Man status. It was not a home in any old-fashioned sense of the word, but a kind of kooky gallery—like a Haight-Ashbury headshop, he decided. Huge posters covered every wall space, ecology boxes like jackdaw collections, strange distorted anatomical drawings. One room was purple shading into a violent crimson, another was black, still another a stark clinical white. The kitchen had a wood-burning stove and a rusty sink cast in the McKinley era. On a wall near the swinging door hung a last year's calendar of the sort stores and insurance companies give away for public relations at Christmastime. But instead of the usual girly or landscape photo, this one was decorated with a reproduction of a page printed in Gothic type. *Gutenberg to Tantra* seemed to be the sponsor's message. Some bookshop, probably. Under the pervasive party odor of pot and incense, Rees could smell mildewed timbers and dry rot here. Poverty syndrome, he thought as he moseyed out again. The richest generation in history playing The Great Depression again as a lifestyle game.

Over the heads of the dancers, he spied Susannah finally, standing on a beachside patio reached through French doors which had been thrown open. With her was a tall blond woman wearing an orange caftan—girl talk, apparently, the woman seemed to be showing Susannah a hat. But in the half-dark, she looked furious. Must be some trick of light, Rees decided as he made his way slowly toward the door, aware now of his unsteadiness. But Susannah looked odd, too. Shocked. Something. Time for rescue anyway, he thought happily.

But by the time he reached the patio, they had disappeared. So much for the savior bit. They were probably trying on dresses by now. Or clawing each other. Sagging into one of the plastic and aluminum chaise longues scattered around the patio, Rees breathed in deeply, finding the fresh sea air as tart as vinegar after the pungency inside. From where he was sitting, Santa Monica Pier looked in the distance like a docked liner, lights on, ready to sail. Imagining a long peaceful voyage, he dozed until his chair rocked, pitching him awake again. "Hey! Oh, it's you—"

Perched precariously beside him, she smiled, her face radiant under the wide-brimmed, sequin-trimmed, black straw hat.

"Susannah," he whispered, reaching for her. "Susannah, Susannah"—loving her name.

Their lips touched but so lightly that he could scarcely feel the contact. Delicately as a cat's, the tip of her tongue touched his mouth, following the contour of his lips around and around until the skin felt seared. God, he kept thinking. God, God. It's going to be. All right. The season of loneliness was over.

TWELVE

It was barely light when Casey wakened—one of those chilly overcast June mornings that send tourists home full of slanderous complaints about Southern California weather. Nesting mockingbirds squawked in the ugly old pines that lined his street. Somewhere a courting dove called mournfully, *Where are you?* Casey smiled at the ceiling, his imagination furnishing a clear picture of Ms. Joanna Hill across a restaurant table this evening. They would toast themselves with nectar, dine on ambrosia. And for dessert, what else but sweet kisses, et cetera? I hope, Casey thought. Oh, wow, do I hope.

Yawning, stretching until his muscles creaked, he looked at the clock. Ten after five, a wide-open temptation to an extra half hour's daydreaming. But if he didn't get up now he risked not finishing his reports before the morning rundown. And Lieutenant Timms was a stickler about keeping the paperwork current.

Promising himself that when *he* made sergeant he would do his share of the clerical drudgery instead of leaving it all to his junior partner, Casey jumped out of bed, padding barefoot through the quiet house to the kitchen, where he plugged in the coffeepot. The dogs whined as usual on the back porch, but they'd have to wait the twelve and a half minutes—no margin for error or indecision—which was all the time he allowed himself for shaving and dressing. Squeezing orange juice took another couple of minutes, and by then the coffee was perking, two slices of bread almost browned in the toaster.

The dogs scratched frantically to get in, and the youngest one, Bimbo, was tuning up to bark. Braced for their assault, Casey slid through the door to the back porch, and shushing the canine hysteria which greeted him, let the three dogs out into the fenced backyard. Bimbo ran in lunatic circles. But the other two sedately traveled from shrub to shrub, happily unaware of the several kinds of patented dog repellent with which his parents regularly sprayed their garden. Serves 'em good and right, Casey thought unkindly. If they insist on giving house room to every flea-bitten stray that wanders down the street—

A thought struck him like a revelation. The dogs were surrogate grandchildren? Imagining his mother's outrage if he suggested such an idea to her, Casey grinned. He had long since learned to keep his theories to himself, for although hip to Freud, his parents were offended by any analysis of themselves or their motives. From me anyway, Casey amended fairly. A son's wisdom doth not a sage make.

Trotting down the driveway, he scooped up the morning *Times* lying on the front lawn. Two more planes had been hijacked. In Belfast the trouble went on. Spreading the newspaper on the tile drainboard, Casey leafed through it quickly while he gulped orange juice and crunched toast, waiting for his coffee to cool. There was only a small item about the Barrett case which last night's *Evening Outlook* had featured as headline news—HIT AND RUN DEATH MURDER SAY POLICE. No mention of counterfeiting. As a local resident, Susannah Roche had received some free publicity, but Paul Rees's name had been left out.

An ex-con, Casey thought. Three years for manslaughter. Felony. Which meant a merciful judge and extenuating circumstances, or a capital charge which a clever attorney had managed to get reduced in exchange for a guilty plea...

"I say let's drop on him," Krug had insisted last night. "Right now, the quicker the better. Even if he's clean on everything else, we got him cold—"

"Not so fast," Timms stopped him. "You're jumping the gun, Al. Picking up Rees isn't going to accomplish anything now."

"How d'you figure that? The way I see it, it's two birds with one stone. We give him protection if he needs it, and we got him on ice—"

But Timms kept shaking his head. "No, we've got to wait till we talk to San Francisco. No use going in blind, maybe scaring him off. He's still the only real witness we've got."

"Some witness," Krug had answered, and for the second time that day, Casey had been inclined to agree with him. But this morning, he wasn't so sure. A guilty man, a parole breaker, wouldn't have stuck his neck out the way Rees had. No man on the run deliberately involves himself in anything which will also involve the police.

Five-thirty, according to the clock on the stove. By pushing the traffic lights a bit he could make it to the station in seven and a half minutes, maybe even less this early. But in deference to its middle-class, early-morning quiet, Casey spared his own street the howling screech of his customary high-speed departure. The residents along the rest of his route did not fare so well, however.

"Heard you highballing that Mustang two miles off," a night-tour man named Smithers said as Casey pounded up the stairs, slid into the squad room and checked the clock. "Real hotdog stuff."

"Hi, Smitty." Casey beamed triumphantly. "Seven minutes exactly, door to door!" He glanced around the squad room. "You get stuck here all night while everybody sacked in?"

"Quit kidding. We've had two stickups, a break-in, a rape and last but not least, a jumper. Call came in about half an hour ago. Some dame with the shakes so bad she could hardly talk. Claimed she heard this screaming, so she got out of bed and looked out the window. Surprise, surprise, there's a body splattered all over the pavement outside."

Suicide. Casey glanced at the call sheet. The woman who had reported it was a Mrs. Elizabeth Hale. Identity of the victim was as yet unknown. But the address rang a bell. Scrambling through his notes from yesterday, Casey checked to make sure. Then he started running.

"Hey, where you going?" Smitty yelled after him.

But by then Casey was already gone.

THIRTEEN

ight from somewhere stabbed through his eyelids. The bathroom, Rees thought groggily, and groaning, rolled over on the tangled bedsheets, drifting again on the edges of sleep. Then he sat up abruptly, listening. No sound from the bathroom. "Hey," he called softly. "Good morning." No answer.

Staggering up, squinting in the glare, he peered into the bathroom. No Susannah there. And the light was not electric but gray hazy daylight let in through the pebbled window he had forgotten to close last night. Oh, lovely, he thought, smiling. An earful was had by the neighbors, no doubt. *Ooo-wow-you-scare-me*. That'll be the day, he decided as he cranked the window closed; the man doesn't live who can scare Susannah.

Yawning and stretching, Rees turned toward the mirror, gasping as he saw it written there in blood across his hangover face. But after the first shock, he realized the red was lipstick: *Ooo-wow-you-scare-me* had been scrawled across the medicine cabinet mirror in wavering capitals. Oh, Susannah.

Laughing hurt his head, but Rees laughed anyway, leaning on the basin. And drinking glass after glass of water, he savored the message. A private joke now. Our joke, he thought happily. Susannah's and mine.

His watch lying on the nightstand said nearly seven. She must have left only a couple of hours ago. He decided that it was like her somehow to slip away like this. And her apartment was only a couple of blocks north on Ocean Avenue. They couldn't go there, she had told him last night. Rees had not asked why—or cared then.

The bed seemed to swing gently under him as he lay back, his mind swarming with images of her lithe, greedy, predatory body clamped to his as if she had grown out of him, the succubus of some insatiable and exhausting dream. The new breed of woman, he thought, laughing and unsentimental, utterly free.

Suppressing the vague distress this idea roused in him, he slipped into sleep, then was instantly awake again, conscious of something trying to surface in his mind. Something about last night. Susannah laughing. *What you can't see...*But that was earlier, over dinner; no laughing then. So it was later on? At the party. *Jervis boozes like it's going out of style tomorrow, too.*

A dim impression of a bearded, pasty middle-aged face with staring eyes swam out of his murky recollections. *Say good night to your host, Paul...*That was it. They were leaving, and the man came plunging out of the crush of dancers muttering something cryptic about "M." Something had been found. And Susannah laughing, yes, she knew. *Play it for giggles, Jervy, keep living dangerously.* Then they were out in the dark, twining like snakes in the car. *Can't go to my place...*Because someone would be there waiting?

Spoiler, Rees thought, staring gritty-eyed at the ceiling. He had no claim on her, so why torment himself as if he did? But he couldn't stop thinking. *Play it for giggles.*

Sick, dizzy, he swung his legs over the side of the bed, sitting with his head in his hands until the hangover vertigo passed. Drinking. Another parole violation. Reaching for the phone on the bedside table, he waited tensely until a sleepy voice answered, "Office," and he gave Susannah's number. Let her be awake, he thought as it rang once at the other end. Let her be there alone. Two rings. Damn, he'd forgotten her call service, and at this hour they would answer fast. Another half ring sounded, then the line was open. No one spoke, but he could hear breathing. "Susannah?"

"Who's this?" a rasping male voice demanded.

"Sorry, I must have the wrong—"

"No, you don't. Who is this?"

"None of your damn business," Rees said furiously. "Let me talk to—"

"Not so fast, mister. And not so smart either. This is Detective Sergeant Krug, Santa Monica Police Department. Been an accident here. Now you gonna tell me who you are, or shall I start guessing?"

FOURTEEN

"No, I didn't say that, I said *almost* dark. I mean, if it'd been really dark, I couldn't have seen—seen—Oh, my God, it was so *aw*ful—!"

"Take it easy, ma'am," Krug said soothingly. "We know it was a shock, all we're trying to find out now is approximate time."

"Well, it must've been about five. I didn't look at the clock. Just barely getting light, anyway. I was sound asleep, of course. What woke me up, you see, was the screaming. You never *heard* such a sound! Horrible. And it went on and on..."

"Must've yelled all the way down," the night-tour detective who answered the squeal had reported as soon as Casey arrived on the scene. "Got six people so far say they heard the screaming. All of 'em live on this side of the building, so it's probably straight."

The body was in the ambulance sitting in the wide concrete drive on the south side of the high-rise apartment building. Tenants in bathrobes clustered near the lobby entrance, watching the ambulance attendants swabbing up the huge pool of blood. *Wouldn't think a human body could hold that much*, the rubbernecks would be telling it later at the office, the shop, the beauty parlor. *Worst thing I ever saw.* But that doesn't keep them from looking, Casey thought. Public appetite for gore seemed insatiable.

"You take a look at the remains?" the night-tour man was asking.

"Not yet."

"Nearly puked myself. Christ, what a way to do it. I figure ten stories or higher. Maybe from the roof. That's seventeenth floor on this one. How long you figure it'd take to fall that far?"

An eternity, Casey thought with a clench of horror in the pit of his stomach. Not like a dream of falling, where you float down and down harmlessly. No, a rushing plunge and the ground coming up as you shriek and shriek and claw the air—

"Not positive yet," the other detective was saying, "but a fast check of the upper floors makes 1005 the only one missing so far. Manager took a look, but with the head bashed in like that, could be anybody. Somebody off the street even."

"What's the name?" Casey asked. "The tenant in 1005."

"Roach, I think he said. Female, anyway."

"Susannah Roche. About five-six. Gray eyes. Long dark hair."

"Well, the hair's right—what's left of it, that is. Sounds like you knew her."

Remembering that the night-tour man had been on sick report for two days, Casey thought of explaining, but there was no time for fill-ins: Krug had to be called immediately. "Tell you later," he said. "Don't let anybody in her apartment," he called back over his shoulder as he rushed off. "Better separate anybody who knows anything—"

Krug was there in twenty minutes, unshaven and red-eyed, savagely impatient with the onlookers still hanging around. "Get the names of anybody with anything sensible to say," he snarled at the nearest patrolman, "and tell the rest of those turds to get back in their apartments, or we're charging every one of 'em with interference." Then he rounded on Casey. "You got the manager and that dame who reported it stashed some place handy?"

"Both in their apartments, Al. Night-squad guy's holding the fort in 1005."

"You call the lab yet?"

"They're on the way. I've got a list from the manager of all the tenants in adjacent apartments. So far there's only one—a woman who was up feeding her baby—who heard anything that might've come from 1005."

They talked to the neighboring tenants one by one then, starting with the young mother who seemed confused and distracted by the squalling of her newborn baby in the bedroom. "If only my husband was here," she kept saying helplessly. "Everything happens at once, it's too much for me! First the baby, and then his father has a heart attack. I mean, his first duty should be here, shouldn't it? But he just fell apart when his mother called—"

They had leased their apartment—1006—only two months ago, she explained, and what with her condition then, she hadn't paid much attention to any neighbors. But of course she had seen the girl in 1005 in the hall once in a while, and a couple of times in the elevator. A model, she had decided, or an actress. Certainly nobody—as she had told her husband—she could ever imagine herself getting really friendly with later.

"She do much entertaining you could hear?" Krug asked.

"Well, no, not much. No parties, anything like that. But sometimes she played records awfully loud. I guess it was records. Anyway, rock stuff. Sometimes late, too. Came right through the walls of our bedroom—"

"How about last night? You hear anything like voices or music last night?"

"N-no, I don't think so. But around three I thought I heard somebody come in. It's so quiet, see, and I was sitting up in bed feeding the baby."

"Hear anybody talking?"

"No, nothing like that. Just the door closing, and somebody moving around in there. I mean, I'm not all that snoopy I listen to be listening. But these new buildings, you can hear everything. Some man upstairs has even complained about the baby already, and I've only been home from the hospital—"

"You're sure about the time?" Casey interrupted. "Three o'clock?"

She sighed exhaustedly. "You wouldn't ask that if you knew anything about babies. He's like an alarm clock. Starts fussing every night the same time. But even if he didn't, I'd wake up. It's the pressure, you see. When you breast-feed, it builds up—"

Except for the occupant of 1004, a stockbroker who was gone by six every morning to catch the opening of the New York Exchange—seven o'clock on the West Coast because of the time differential—they covered the other tenants on the tenth floor. Then they went on to Mrs. Hale, who was still shaking, still almost incoherent, but positive all the same that it was barely light when she had heard the screaming. After leaving the Hale apartment on the first floor, they rode the elevator back up to the tenth. A patrolman guarded the door of 1005; inside they could hear the voices of the technicians. As the cop opened the door for them, they heard the telephone. Krug was across the room in two long strides, grabbing it on the third ring.

"Guess who," he said as he hung up. "I told Timms we should nail that guy. You"—he pointed to a fresh-faced rookie patrolman standing just inside the door—"get over to the Pelican Motel and baby-sit with a guy named Rees—Paul Joseph Rees— till we get there."

"Yes, sir." The rookie hesitated. "But what'll I tell him, Sergeant?"

Krug groaned. "For Chrissake, don't they teach you guys anything at the Academy anymore? Tell him any damn thing you want, just keep him there. Now get moving!"

The rookie disappeared.

"You guys on round-the-clock duty too, I see," McGregor, the senior laboratory technician, commented bitterly. "You know it was almost midnight by the time we finished with that Mercedes last night?"

"Tough luck, Mac." Krug sucked his teeth, surveying the small pop-style living room furnished in molded plastic and bean-bag chairs in op-art colors. White shutters closed off all but one of the south-facing windows—a casement which stood wide open. "That the window she went out of?"

"That's the one."

"No screen," Casey commented when McGregor opened the shutters, revealing a wide stationary pane flanked by tall casements on either side. "The other window has one, I see."

"Somebody unhooked it and took it down," McGregor said. "Watch that shoe." They carefully stepped around the white sandal lying on the floor near the window. "Figure she lost it going out. They usually take their shoes off for some reason, but it don't look like this one bothered."

"Any sign it could've been an accident?" Krug inquired. "Or maybe she had help?"

The lab man shrugged. "We got a couple marks here—" He pointed with his pencil to two small gouges in the wall below the window embrasure. "Could be a heel did those. Could be furniture, too. Or somebody careless with a vacuum cleaner. If somebody pushed her, you got trouble, Al."

"Convince me."

"Well, for starters, why no hand marks around the window? Gouges in the carpet? Anybody fighting for their life, stands to reason they'll be stomping and clawing every which way. But there isn't a sign of a struggle."

"Okay, where's this window screen?"

"Behind the door in the bedroom." McGregor grinned. "And there goes your accident theory."

"So maybe a window washer forgot it. Make a note to ask the manager," Krug instructed Casey. "While we're at it, we better find out whether she was late on her rent, any money problems he might know about."

Casey was still scribbling in his notebook when the lieutenant arrived. In his usual fashion on a new case, Timms walked around with his hands in his pockets while Krug filled him in. "Coincidence," he kept muttering. "The sudden death of a witness in a homicide case. *Jesus*," he exploded, "even if it is suicide, we'll have to prove it! And if it's accident, our necks are really in a sling. No coroner's inquest is going to sit still for anything but concrete proof there's no connection when they hear she's on record in that Barrett mess."

Glum-faced, he turned to the other detectives who had arrived with him. "Everyone in the building must be questioned," he instructed, "help as well as tenants. Find out when trash was collected, milk was delivered. Find out when the *Times* delivery-man usually gets here in the morning. With the tenants, find out who was out and how late. Find out if anybody saw her in the halls or the elevator—

"You know the drill," he added impatiently. "What we're looking for is anything and everything right now. Hopefully somebody who saw her coming home. Somebody who can fix time as near exact as possible. And I want every detail called in to me the minute you get anything. We'll keep a running collation of what everybody comes up with. Suicide or no, we've got to hit this like a ton of bricks."

"Ton of shit, he means," Krug muttered to Casey as the others dispersed. "One ripe possible we got, you want to bet we leave him out there hanging on the tree?"

"Nobody's leaving anything hanging," Timms snapped. "Smitty's doing a fast check of the Pelican Motel right now, and as soon as he knows anything, we'll hear." He disappeared into the bedroom.

After an instant's hesitation, Krug followed with Casey at his heels. Silently, Timms pointed out the wrinkled depression in the fake-fur spread on the bed. Two pillows were propped against the wall at the head, rumpled from the weight of someone leaning against them.

"Cigar smoker flopped there," McGregor, the lab man, reported. "Got three butts from the ashtray on the nightstand. We'll vacuum for hair samples on the pillows, anything we can find in that fake fur. We've already started on the latents. I'll get the photographing done before we start moving stuff." He grinned at Krug. "Little cigars, Al. Like you smoke. You sure you haven't been making time on the sly?"

"Yeah, in my dreams I'm a big lover. Speaking of that," Krug added, "I'll try offering a smoke to Rees when we see him. Be interesting to know when he left here last night."

"You didn't tell me he admitted he was here," Timms said.

"He didn't. But I'll lay you even money we'll find his prints all over this place."

One look at him and they knew the rookie must have spilled the beans. Appearing sick and shaky, shrunken somehow, he sat in an armchair in the corner of the motel room, his shirt and trousers wrinkled, obviously thrown on, his hair uncombed.

He had barely managed to catch him, the rookie had reported outside when Casey and Krug arrived at the motel; Rees was in his Volkswagen, ready to drive off, and only the threat of arrest had stopped him.

"Skipping," Krug had said.

"No, sir, I don't think so. He kept yelling about an accident—"

"You tell him she's dead?"

Red-faced, the rookie had stared at Krug mutely.

"Okay, catch up with your partner, we'll take over here."

The motel room smelled of smoke and vomit. Someone had pulled up the counterpane without making the bed, Casey noticed.

"Hear you had company last night," Krug was saying. "According to the people on either side of you here, it was a woman. You want to tell us who she was?"

"You already know," Rees said dully.

"Yeah, I guess we do, but we'd like you to tell us."

"Susannah Roche."

"Uh-hunh. So she spent the night here?"

"A few hours, yes."

"Yeah, we heard about those few hours. Okay, then what? You took her home, I guess."

"No, I was asleep when she—she—" A spasm distorted his face suddenly, and he masked it with his hands. "Oh, Jesus," they heard him whisper, "what in God's name *happened?*"

They took him to the station for a brief questioning, then left him alone in the interrogation room and trudged upstairs to the Detective Bureau. Lieutenant Timms was back also, but on the phone when they walked in, so Casey made a fast trip down the stairs again to the coffee-vending machine.

"This's got sugar in it," Timms complained after the first sip. "Yours, Al." They switched cups. "All right, what'd you get out of Rees so far?"

"Mostly a big act how shocked he is." Krug gulped his coffee, shuddering. "Christ, what do they make this stuff out of, ground-up tennis shoes? They had a dinner date, he claims, and went on to some party. We'll check it out later. Then they came back to his motel and balled for a while. No reason he knows of for her to dive out the window."

"You didn't give him any hints we're doing a full-scale investigation?" Timms smiled at Krug's expression. "All right, Al, just checking. Even an old dog can miss a trick now and then. He give you any indication he might've known her before?"

"Only since yesterday." Krug grunted. "Same old crap about it's an ill wind, I guess."

"Yeah, a fast worker, this guy. All right, what about times?"

"Well, he's either fuzzy or faking on that one. Have to dig some more, I guess. Guy in the room next to Rees's heard 'em roll in about two, but that's all he could tell us. Rees claims he was asleep when she left."

"Some lover," Timms snorted. "My day, it was the men who put their pants back on and did the disappearing act. You hit him at all on the parole business?"

"Not yet. Figured we'd save that for later."

"Good. I'll call San Francisco now. With any luck, he's a violator, which means we can keep him on ice till we make some connections."

While Timms was on the phone, Casey made another fast trip downstairs with the information Rees had given them about the clothing Susannah Roche had been wearing last evening.

"A sleeveless dress, a groovy print," the morgue attendant repeated after him. "Check, we got it. Heeled sandals, white. We got one. The other's probably still at the scene. Same with the black hat." He grinned at Casey, whose weak stomach was well known. "Want to see the body? No? Sure? It's a nice one—but kind of accordion-pleated." He laughed as Casey gulped. "Don't puke on the help, it's bad for interdepartmental relations. You want time of death, I suppose, right to the minute. Well, stick around. So far all we've got is prints, measurements, the usual. Lab's got everything. With any luck you'll have a make by this afternoon."

"No problem there—we're pretty sure who she is. All we need is a formal identification."

"Well, bring a bucket with whoever's elected, because there's nothing left of her head but the stalk. And the—Hey, where you going?" he called after Casey. "Listen, I haven't even started on the good part yet…"

"His PO in San Francisco is a guy named Stevens," Lieutenant Timms reported. "Jake Stevens. According to him, Rees is clean so far. Seems he requested a transfer to LA Parole Authority a month ago, and the clearance came through Monday, May twenty-ninth. Rees supposedly left the San Francisco area the same day, driving. He's due to report to his new PO down here tomorrow."

"It's a one-day trip from Frisco," Krug said. "So what took him so long? He told us he only got here Friday. That's four days to drive less than five hundred miles."

"Well, maybe he stopped along the way, Al. Check it out, anyway. You clear the clothing list yet?" he asked Casey.

"Yes, sir. Couple items missing but they're probably at the scene."

"Mac'll have it all listed," Krug predicted. "Down to the last piece of fuzz on the carpet. This guy Stevens give with any dope about lover boy's felony rap?"

Timms nodded. "Sounds like a bad break to me. But you never know. Could be a good lawyer instead of extenuating circumstances." He leaned back in his swivel chair, a storyteller now. "Seems a couple years ago, Rees let his wife out of the car—to mail a letter or something—and when she crossed the street some nut ran the signal and knocked her down with his pickup truck. On top of that, the guy tried to run. But a witness chased him in his own car and cut him off. Okay! So the wife is DOA by the time the ambulance gets there. And the hit-and-runner's got a felony tag, of course. But by the time he gets to court, he's got a blackout story worked up, and some lawyer like Belli to tell it for him. You know the result—haven't you seen it enough? The guy gets off with a slap on the wrist and a nice little suspension—"

"And Rees goes ape?"

"You guessed it, Al. According to Stevens, he attacked the ex-defendant outside the courtroom. Knocked him clear down a flight of stairs. Marble ones. Result, a broken neck, the guy's dead as a mackerel."

"Tough luck," Krug said grudgingly. "But it still makes him a rough customer, a guy who blows his stack like that."

"I agree, Al. So the question now is, Could he do it again? The only way we'll find out is to push him till he cracks."

FIFTEEN

They kept asking the same questions, reworded, rephrased, working patiently as weavers across the pattern of his evening with Susannah. Time seemed to obsess them—When had he picked her up at her apartment? Exactly what time had they walked out the door? How long had they spent dining at the Ultimate Perception? What time had they arrived at the beach-house party? When had they left? What was the last time Rees had looked at his watch?—on and on. "I keep telling you," he said exhaustedly, "I can't say exactly. We weren't on any kind of schedule."

"Get as near as you can."

"But why does it matter?" Rees asked the young detective, but.

It was Krug who answered. "Just take our word, it does."

Hoisting a haunch onto the corner of the table nearest Rees, Krug fished in a breast pocket, producing a thin, narrow carton and opening the flap. "Smoke?" he offered.

"No, thanks, I don't use cigars."

"Un-hunh." Krug glanced at his partner. "You want to part with one of your gaspers, Casey?"

"Sure, why not?" He offered a pack of Carltons, and Rees took one gratefully.

Krug lit it and his own small cigar with a kitchen match he snapped alight with his thumbnail. "Okay," he said, puffing, "it's about four, you think, maybe four-thirty this morning when you go to sleep, right? And she's tucked in there with you, no worries about getting home. So then what?"

"I don't know," Rees said miserably. "She seemed so happy. I can't believe anything was preying on her mind. It can't be suicide! She wasn't—"

"Mr. Rees," Casey stopped him. "She was an actress. And you said yourself you hardly knew her."

"But she wasn't that sort of—"

"Okay, okay," Krug interrupted, "let's go on." He blew a plume of smoke just over Rees's head. "She a good lay?" he asked softly. "Kicky, maybe? Little whory?"

"Go to hell!"

"Ah come on, fella, you only knew her the one day. Isn't as if she was your steady." Krug hitched himself closer. "So you ball maybe an hour at your place, right? Then you catch your breath and try some new tricks at her place—" Rees kept shaking his head, but Krug went bulldozing on: "How many times did you do it? Two? Three? Don't just sit there wagging your head, lover boy. Tell us what happened."

"I'm trying to," Rees said hoarsely, suppressing his rage. "I *have* told you." He blinked at Krug dizzily, seeing him double for an instant. "Look, I don't know what you're trying to get at with all this. I told you I was asleep when she left, so I don't know what happened." He hesitated, but neither detective spoke. "You're right, I suppose," he went on quietly. "I didn't know her at all. But I can't believe I couldn't have sensed it if she was troubled. Sensed something, anyway." His voice cracked and he swallowed a lump. "We'd had a lot to drink. And she couldn't see very well. She could've opened the window and—and lost her balance—" But there was no response, and helpless, baffled, he gave up.

Krug kept puffing, staring impassively at some point just behind Rees. His partner seemed lost in thought also, and the silence in the ugly, almost bare room expanded. Then abruptly Casey said, "Mr. Rees, we've been wondering why you didn't level with us yesterday." His glance was mild, but Rees was not fooled. He realized now why they were questioning him like a criminal.

"Maybe you didn't realize we'd check up on you? It's standard procedure."

"Pretty low standards," Rees said bitterly. "Wouldn't a phone call have been easier than all that hocus-pocus with my luggage?"

Krug leaned toward him, puffing smoke in his face. "What hocus-pocus you talking about?"

"Slitting linings, messing everything around. For God's sake, even my shaving kit—!"

"Wait a minute," Krug stopped him. "You saying your room was searched?"

Rees ground his teeth. "Don't worry, Sergeant, I'm not silly enough to think it would do any good to complain. I know my limitations as a parolee. Keep my nose clean and my mouth shut. All the privileges are on your side now."

"Well, there's a poser," Lieutenant Timms said later when they reported upstairs. "You checked, of course."

"Damn right we checked," Krug said furiously. "Hustled him back to the Pelican, and sure enough—" He blew out his breath. "So what's it mean? All it takes is a razor blade. Sly bastard could've done it himself."

"Possible, I suppose. So the next question is why." Timms chewed his lower lip. "You trying for any prints?"

"Yeah, we brought him and the stuff back here. Two suitcases and a shaving rig. Lab's got it now." Then he glared at Casey. "Okay, speak your piece and get it over with. This guy's still harping about protection."

"For Rees you mean?"

Casey nodded. "Seems like negligence on our part if we don't at least consider it, Lieutenant. Because if someone did search his luggage—"

"When did he say he noticed it first?"

"Yesterday, in the afternoon."

"Could be coincidence—he had a thief in there." Timms steepled his fingers, leaning his chin on the peak the tips made. "Check the manager at the Pelican. Chances are if they had a sneak around there, he'd hit more than one room."

"That fella's really got a complex," the motel manager said irritably. "Not enough he bothers me with it, now he's got to call cops. Told him yesterday I'd keep that wad of money in the safe here for him. Look at that—" He pointed toward the rear of the small office and a safe like an old-fashioned blued-steel stove. "Couldn't want better protection. But no, he's got to carry it with him, flash the roll around. I tell you, some fellas just don't have half sense, picking up women and carrying on the way they do. I try to protect my guests, but you can't protect a man that won't have it." He paused, squinting, apparently never in need of breath. "Say, one of my regulars—he stops here a couple times every month—had the unit next to Rees. Anyway, he told me you was asking about him earlier. Some woman he had in there with him last night. Must be the same one messed up the mirror. Maid was in here bellyaching about it before I even got a chance to eat my breakfast. They like to get in the units fast— you know how they are. Anybody goes out early for breakfast or something, they're in there like a shot. That way the units don't stack up on 'em around checkout time later. Anyhow! She comes in crying about this lipstick all over the mirror in Number Eleven. That's Rees's unit. Had to use kerosene to get it off. 'You scare me.' Can y'imagine the kind of woman writes that all over a man's mirror? 'You scare me.' "He chuckled breathlessly. "Maybe he did, too! Place was a mess for sure. Had a real bang-up time in there from two on, according to the guy next door. Windows wide open and just a-going at it. If he paid her, he must've really owed her plenty, getting a time like that out of her..."

CAROLYN WESTON

"It was a joke," Rees said. "Somebody kept yelling it at the party. 'Ooo-wow-you-scare-me.' So I suppose Susannah—" his voice trailed off. The reality of death nullified humor. "How long are you going to keep me sitting here? I'm not charged with anything, so you can't—"

"Keep your shirt on, Mr. Rees, we're not finished yet." Krug eyed him calmly. "The manager at the Pelican told us you're carrying a wad of dough. Like maybe a couple, three thousand or more? Says you squawked yesterday about somebody in your room, but you wouldn't let him keep it in the safe for you."

Trying to conceal his shock, Rees forced himself to keep looking at Krug. He had not guessed that they would talk to the motel manager, too. With a skidding sensation that he was headed for disaster, he said casually, "It isn't that much money. But after I noticed that my luggage had been searched—"

"You had the money on you?"

Either way he answered, Rees realized, the question was a trap. For if they had discovered the shoe box yesterday, he dared not lie. And if they hadn't, the truth that the money was winnings from gambling would inevitably lead to the next question, *Where?* Stateline, Nevada. "If you mean," he began carefully, "was anything taken—"

"That wasn't the question, Mr. Rees," Casey interrupted. "The point is, if your room was searched and the money was there, that could suggest something about the thief."

"If there was a thief." Krug grinned at Rees. "Maybe you've changed your mind about your room getting tossed?"

"I haven't changed my mind about anything, Sergeant. All I meant was, if nothing was stolen—"

"Uh-hunh. Okay, Mr. Rees." Krug leaned back, looking up at the high fluorescent tubes which filled the interrogation room with cold, bright, shadowless light. "Seems funny, an ex-con with a lot of dough. Don't it seem funny to you, Casey?"

"Mr. Rees is one of the lucky ones, I guess."

"That's for sure. Most guys get out, all they got is the clothes on their back and twenty-five bucks."

One of the lucky ones, Rees thought hopelessly, listening to them. Even as winner, he was a loser. The bitter realization was bitterer still when he remembered his elation at that Tahoe dice table, his sudden foolish conviction as he had bet and won, kept doubling and winning, that some corner had been turned, that he was finally out of the darkness that had shrouded his life. Aware that both detectives were looking at him—waiting, he guessed, for some explanation as to why he was carrying such a sum—he told them that he had sold his house in San Francisco, his furniture, too. Yes, a good deal of cash was involved because furnishings were chattel and didn't go through escrow. As he talked his fever soared, he couldn't stop himself talking. And he knew that if they checked more than superficially, they would soon see the flaw in his apparent truthfulness.

"Looks like you don't believe in banks," Krug said finally. "Didn't your PO squawk when you told him you were leaving town with all that cash on you?"

"No, he—Well, actually I didn't tell him. He knew I was solvent, so we never bothered discussing money matters."

"Okay, Mr. Rees." Abruptly, Krug stood up. "We'll get started on your statement now. While you're waiting to sign it you might as well make an identification for us. Kill two birds with one stone that way. Maybe save you another trip back here later."

SIXTEEN

Slowly, disoriented, he followed sidewalks, passing the Sears store he had seen yesterday, crossing Colorado, continuing on Second, which, in this part of Santa Monica, seemed to be a backwater of garages, small repair shops and real estate offices. Traffic on the street seemed ominously slow, every vehicle a surveillance car tracking his movements. And the people he looked at through store windows appeared shadowy, furtive, contaminated by the same evil which had taken root in his life. Ordinariness was a lie, Rees realized now, a shallow one-dimensional illusion concealing a vast landscape of violence and terror. And no matter how he might long to believe otherwise, once having seen behind the lie, there was no return to innocence.

At the corner of Broadway he paused, blinking dizzily in the hazy sunlight. The thing he had seen in the morgue swam monstrously behind his eyes—a heap of bloody flesh and broken bones with no head, no face. An inhuman thing, and they said it was Susannah. Couldn't be. But it had her hands. It had her feet. In the center of his mind, she leaned blindly out the window. *Screamed all the way down*, Krug had said. *Play it for giggles.* Out and down. Screaming into oblivion.

Stumbling, he stepped off the curb, bumping a pedestrian coming the other way—a middle-aged man who muttered furiously, "Drunk. Cops ought to get you bums off the street." A jowly, outraged fatcat face.

Hatred stirred in Rees like a puff of smoke out of a heap of ashes. These are our judges and protectors. Then the flicker of fury blew out, leaving a familiar empty hopelessness. Even the freedom to move on, to forget, was denied him.

"You got a date tomorrow, don't forget," Krug had reminded him. "I guess you know if you leave this area without reporting to the Parole Authority you're in violation?" And as Rees nodded he had smiled, saying softly, "Yeah, sure you do. Okay, be seeing you, Mr. Rees." A promise. A threat. His mean man's grin was the last thing Rees had seen as he had walked out.

Susannah, what happened?

Feeling hollow, light-headed, Rees turned west toward the glare of the sea, passing pawnshops, beer joints, forlorn-looking beaneries with hand-lettered signs in the windows advertising breakfast and lunch specials. Two winos sat sleeping on the bus-stop bench with their heads lolling back as if they had been half-decapitated. Shaking, Rees slid by them, stopping at the corner across from the park which skirted the palisades. He was only a couple of blocks from the motel now. Five minutes away. But the idea of returning filled him with dread. Not yet, he thought. Not ever, he meant. There was a bar at the corner and he went in.

SEVENTEEN

In the sheaf of overnight reports they had missed seeing earlier, Krug discovered a citizen complaint from the old man who had rented his garage to the deceased Barrett. "Don't believe this," he muttered. " 'Subject demands return of impounded Mercedes'? This guy's got to be dingy! Better call him," he advised Casey. "Old bastard probably figures he can sue us for something." He would meet Casey downstairs in ten or fifteen minutes...

"You fellas are really costing me some money," the old man squawked. "I phoned there last night, but the dumbhead I talked to couldn't give me any satisfaction."

"What was it you wanted, sir?" Casey inquired politely. "The Mercedes was legally impounded."

"Who says it was! I got no receipt or nothing, and here's his brother calling me—"

"When was this, sir?"

"Got me out of bed last night. Said he was from out of town. Say, what happened to Hower? Way his brother was talking, sounded to me like he's gone or something. Anyhow, this fella said he'd send me the rent."

"Did he mention his name? Where he was calling from?"

Dead silence at the other end, but Casey heard asthmatic breathing. "Come to think of it, he didn't say. Just asked me if he could leave the car for a while till he made arrangements."

"Did you tell him it was impounded?"

"Why sure, I told him. 'Call the cops,' I says. 'And while you're at it, ask 'em how come they taken that car without getting my permission'—"

"Brother, my ass," Krug growled. "He's pretty cute, hah? Murdering bastard. Figured his kill car was safe in the hidey hole. All he had to do was sit tight, pay the rent every month, we'd never find it." He kept sucking his teeth while Casey drove north from Colorado on Ocean Avenue. Thin sunlight burned through the overcast, and the hills overlooking Malibu in the distance were slowly emerging—a herd of monsters sliding into the sea. "Amateurs, sport. Strictly. And it's panic time." Krug blew out his breath. "We got our work cut out for us, that's for sure."

He kept talking, but the words became a meaningless drone to Casey as he mentally picked over the enigmatic pieces. Not even a puzzle yet, he decided. And it could be coincidence. A hit-and-run. Then a suicide? A word from the Academy casebooks rolled sonorously through his mind: defenestration. By exact definition, a throwing out of a person or thing through, or by way of, a window. A window without a screen. But no sign of a struggle.

Unbidden then came the thought that Susannah Roche had been the same age as Joey, and before he could suppress the quick sting of intense response, Casey's breath caught painfully. Don't associate, he reminded himself of Rule Number One. Any policeman who begins to connect what happens to victims with what might happen to loved ones—

"Hey, for Chrissake," Krug protested, "you're passing the building!"

Loved ones. Man, you're overreacting, Casey told himself as he made a U-turn, pulling into the wide drive south of the high rise. Even a girl-freak like you can't make one hamburger lunch and some sexy pipe dreams into a deathless romance. He stopped the Mustang just short of the huge wet stain where the ambulance crew had mopped up.

"Do yourself a favor and get married, lover," Krug, the mind reader, was saying. "Keep your mind on your work, hah? And speaking of that," he added sourly when they had climbed out of the Mustang, "you better hit the manager here again. By now maybe he'll have some bright ideas about that window screen."

But the manager couldn't think about anything, Casey discovered, except upset tenants, the possibility of vacancies resulting from all those cops snooping around. "After all," he said over and over, "this is a *luxury* building. People paying this kind of rent—" A broken record.

"Got zilch," Casey reported half an hour later when he joined Krug in 1005. "Buttons will please use the service elevator, et cetera. But I found out they've got a security guard here nights. An ex-cop named Cooley. Claims he was patrolling the basement at five this morning—the garage and so forth. No traffic in or out he knows about."

"That's a big help."

McGregor, the lab technician, didn't have any helpful news either, it seemed. "Better pull some rabbits out of your hats if you figure on locking this one up as anything but a question mark," he advised them acidly. "For prima facie evidence, we got nothing so far. And brace yourselves, it could stay that way." The lock hadn't been tampered with, he told them, and it was a dead-bolt type. Without a hacksaw, only a pro could get in without a key.

"Or somebody who walked in with her," Krug corrected him. "Or somebody she let in."

"Or somebody who already had a key." McGregor shrugged. "I take it you got a suspect?"

"We're working on it."

"The manager claims there hasn't been a window washer around for over a month," Casey said. "So that screen's something to think about, too."

"Possible." McGregor nodded. "On the other hand, if you're trying the crime-of-passion route, it don't go so good with a guy who carefully gets the screen out of the way and hides it in the bedroom."

"Passion, for Chrissake," Krug groaned.

While they bickered amiably, Casey wandered into the kitchen, inspecting the dirty dishes in the sink—a coffee mug, the glass portion of a blender stained with a fruity-smelling concoction—yesterday's diet breakfast, he guessed. Did Joey live like this? With an unconscious smile, Casey studied the lipstick stain on the rim of the mug, touching it lightly with one forefinger. Then shocked at himself—this girl was a corpse, after all—he replaced the mug in the sink. Keep your mind on your work.

The refrigerator contained only some low-fat milk, a wedge of cheese, a bottle of apple juice guaranteed to be free of preservatives and pressed from the freshest organically grown fruit and a huge supply of drink mixers. On the tile drainboard lay a pair of heavy tinted spectacles with huge rims. Bug-eye shades, Casey thought. Essential equipment for your compleat mod. But when he tried them on idly, he had a visual shock, for the smoked lenses were prescription-ground and so strong that they literally blinded him. "Take a look at these, Al," he called. No answer, and Casey peered around the kitchen door into the living room.

"In there." McGregor jerked a thumb toward the bedroom. "Getting his jollies with the undies, probably."

Krug had the louvered doors of a long shallow closet open, Casey discovered. "Get a load of this wardrobe. Spent her money on her back, that's for sure."

The closet was filled with clothing, all neatly hung, winter things covered with plastic bags, shoes tidily racked, hats on stands lined up on the shelf overhead. But no black one trimmed with sequins, Casey noticed. Mentally circling it on the list in his mind, he poked among the hangers. "Wonder what happened to that raincoat she was wearing?"

"John she was hoofing it home from probably came by and got it."

Casey showed him the sunglasses. "Remember Rees said she couldn't see very well. If these were hers, we've got our answer why her description of the car was completely off."

But Krug wasn't interested; he kept poking in bureau drawers. "Bound to be an address book here somewhere. All these classy hookers carry 'em. Take a look in the other room."

Casey found his way blocked by Harry Berger, who was lounging in the doorway, hands in his pockets, an I-told-you-so grin creasing his fattish face. "Nice kettle of gefülte fish, right? One witness down, one to go. I told you those pigeons might be headed for our pot."

"Listen to the guy." Krug sighed. "Gets his exercise jumping to conclusions. Harry, we got nothing yet says this is homicide. Turns out she was halfway blind, maybe. Could be she was fooling with the window—"

"You trying to tell me it's coincidence?" Berger looked outraged. "Even a blind man could see the same pattern here," he snarled. A trumped-up accident. Strictly amateur stuff. "You mamzer." He kept glaring at Krug after they told him about the old man's complaint last night. "For sure that was the killer! And his next stop was here. Should've kept her name out of the papers." He puffed out an indignant breath. "This dreck case, how much wilder is it going to get? And time's running out. They've had seven months—give or take a couple for setting up shop. According to the feds, that's more than enough time to manufacture a truckload of those phony twenties."

"Your worry," Krug grunted. "Not ours."

"You mean you hope it is. How about your other witness, Al? You got some protection out for him?"

"For my dough, he's our prime suspect. An ex-con carrying heavy sugar, and he spends last night romancing her?"

Berger looked even more unhappy. "All I'm hoping is you're wrong, and he's innocent as the well-known newborn. Because if he is—well, you figure it. Sooner or later our paperhanging tigers'll come hunting him, too."

"Lambs, tigers, some zoo," Lieutenant Timms snorted when they reported in later. "He's as bad as the feds. Set their mothers up probably, if it'd help 'em make a bust. On the other hand, he's right. If Rees isn't involved—Well, let's check the money angle before we start worrying." He reached for the phone on his desk. "Get me San Francisco Parole Authority," he said into the receiver. "Person-to-person call to Jake Stevens."

While they waited to hear, Casey began typing a report in triplicate, an unwilling audience to Krug's call home to continue what appeared to be a permanent and insoluble argument with his wife about painting their house. Quite obviously Mrs. K was as tough as her husband and equally stubborn. A case of the rock meeting the hard place, Casey thought. Amazing. Some truth perhaps in his mother's old gag about marriages being made in heaven? "All right," Timms's parade-ground boom jolted him. "Got your money answer, you guys."

Krug hung up on his wife and Casey abandoned his typewriter. "Lay you ten to one it's a bummer," Krug muttered as they crossed the squad room to Timms's corner desk. Good old Uncle Al, sniffs the air, divines answers.

"According to Stevens, he's solvent, all right," Timms told them. "But his money's still in San Francisco. Stevens checked while I was still on the line—he's got a buddy in some bank there, so it was easy. Seems Rees only drew out five hundred bucks to travel on, so if he's got any more than that in his possession, you'll have to try to make him account for it."

"Yeah, if he can," Krug said. "And I'll bet a month's salary, any odds, the lying son of a bitch can't."

EIGHTEEN

Although the hazy sun was warm, Rees felt chilled to the bone, uncertain of himself and his motives now that he was here. Could be the wrong place anyway, he thought as he parked in front of the house. Whether it was or not, he should have tried to phone first.

After two slow drinks in the bar on Ocean Avenue, he had returned to the motel, thinking he might sleep or at least shower and shave. But he couldn't bear the antiseptic sterility of the room—no trace of Susannah remaining, but the sense of her there hauntingly, a hoarded image behind the mirror. Dead yet still alive. Like Ellen, he thought, the old sluggish pain of loss sharp again, piercing. And I am alive as usual, yet dead. A carrier of death? The urge to seek even the cold comfort of confirmation, someone who had known Susannah—yes, she was always suicidal—plagued him.

Shivering, a sleepwalker, he had pulled on the coat which matched his wrinkled trousers. He was halfway out the door, fishing in his pockets for the Volkswagen keys, when he thought of the shoe box with its Nevada label. Seems funny, an ex-con with a lot of dough. Cops have X-ray eyes. Tearing up the box lid, he stuffed the pieces into the matching buff-and-black plastic bag. He'd throw it in one of the litter cans in the park across the way. No, too close, he decided. He would toss it out of the car when he was sure no one was watching. But how could he be certain Krug wasn't having him followed? The plastic bag still lay under the driver's seat in the Volkswagen.

In daylight the house looked even shabbier than he remembered, closed and unwelcoming. A truck boomed by on the Coast Highway a few feet from him, and deafened, he crawled awkwardly out the curbside door, bumping into a rural-style mailbox fastened to a thick redwood post. Bolted to the top of the box, he noticed, was a rusty pierced-metal nameplate: *E & J Godwin*. Good thing he hadn't tried calling all the Jervises in the phone book, Rees thought. J for Jervis. E for—

Suddenly his mind jumped back, grasping the significance of Jervis Godwin's cryptic message to Susannah. "M" must be "Em" instead, short for Emily or perhaps Emma. The wife, anyway. And the something which had been found was—the hat?

Play it for giggles, Jervy. Keep living dangerously. What he had observed last night was a jealous confrontation, Rees realized. And feeling spared something unbearable, a fool's errand, he climbed back into the Volkswagen and drove away quickly.

"This guy Rees gets cuter and cuter." Puffing furiously on one of his small smelly cigars, Krug kept flipping pages of the western section of the telephone directory lying on his desk. "The restaurant's here, all right. Ultimate Perception—whatever that means. But there's nobody named Jervis on the Coast Highway."

"Maybe it's Jarvis, Al."

"No soap, I tried it. You think he could've been conning us about that so-called party?"

Casey was typing a report—one less to pin him here at the end of the day if he could finish it—and to stop Krug's distracting conversation, he said, "Could be." But it didn't work.

"Maybe a private number. Listen, you got any girlfriends at the phone company who could find out without a lot of red tape?"

Casey admitted he did. Not a girlfriend exactly, a marriage-hungry ex-schoolmate from Samohi. Reluctantly, he dialed the General Telephone Company and asked for the business office.

"No unlisted Jervises," he reported after he had hung up a few minutes later, stuck now with a luncheon date he'd have to weasel out of later. "No Jarvises either, Al. Looks like he got the name all wrong."

"Fat chance." Krug heaved himself out of his desk chair. "You stick here, I'll bring the son of a bitch in again. Maybe after a couple more trips, he'll finally start talking straight for a change."

Or he'll scare and run, Casey thought as he typed furiously. Good old Uncle Al would like that. Running men simplify a policeman's work.

He had almost finished the report—a race against the telephone and Krug's return—when a woman wearing a shabby-looking black coat walked into the squad room. It was Gerald Barrett's sister. They had forgotten all about her. "You should've called us," Casey told her guiltily as he seated her at Krug's desk, which sat back to back with his own. Someone would have picked her up at the airport. They hadn't meant her to have to fend for herself—

"Don't worry about it," she interrupted coolly. "I'm perfectly able to get around by myself."

Recognizing the no-nonsense tone—a Women's Libber perhaps?—Casey dropped the subject. Where the hell was Krug, he kept wondering while he took down particulars. How the hell long did it take to make a pickup anyway?

"No, that's double *e*," she corrected him. "Shirlee. My mother's name is Shirley, and my father's was Lee. Don't suppose they could resist it." She smiled faintly. "Should be grateful, I guess, they didn't think up something like Petunia."

Erasing *Shirley* with a *y*, Casey took his time printing *Reilly, Shirlee Barrett* again, and her Nebraska address. Damn Al, he was probably feeding his face somewhere. Couldn't stall much more than half an hour, Casey decided. They'd have to view the body, and he lacked whatever ingredient Krug lent to such occasions which kept most viewers of remains from collapsing into hysteria. Two in one day was too many.

"—Rotten reason to make a trip you've dreamed of for years, isn't it," she was saying. "I'd hate to tell you how long I've wanted to come to California. But with six kids and a stick-in-the-mud husband. Well, at least I'm getting a look. Guess it'll have to last me till my kids're grown."

She kept talking, concealing an apprehension Casey could only guess at. A plain woman, years older than her brother, probably one of those thankless mainstays of her family. He told her that the inquest was scheduled for tomorrow at ten o'clock, and inquired gently if she had discussed arrangements with the family.

"Didn't have a chance," she answered bitterly. "Isn't bad enough I spend all this money coming here, she's got to scream the walls down, wanting to bring him home, too. The return of the prodigal to his loving mother." Her eyes filled suddenly. "Oh God," she whispered, "if he had to die, why couldn't he do it decently!" Then she collapsed, sobbing.

Casey rooted for Kleenex in Haynes's desk—a nasal sufferer, Haynes was always good for Kleenex. Then he went after a paper cup of water. But by the time he got back with it, she was composed again.

"Let's get it over with." Sniffing, she stood up, visibly bracing herself. "Nothing's going to make it any easier, is it?"

"I'm afraid not, Mrs. Reilly." Casey took her arm. "This way. It's—he's downstairs."

Krug met them in the corridor—alone, Casey noted, he must have missed out on Rees—and took over from there. But Mrs. Reilly didn't break down after all when she looked at the body in the morgue. Yes, that was her brother, she told them stonily, and looked away. Still frozen, tearless, she signed the formal identification statement upstairs at Krug's desk, and received the itemized list of Barrett's effects, including a notation about the counterfeit bills, which, of course, were not returnable.

The amount struck her first. "All that money…" her voice trailed off as she read on. "You mean it was *fake?*"

"That's right, Mrs. Reilly."

She sagged in the chair. "That's what the rest of it was too, I suppose." Bleakly, she looked from one to the other. "He's been sending money home all these months. Since last December. Never said how he got it, just he was doing great and something big was—Oh, my God, she'll have to pay it all back!"

"If the money was spent," Casey reassured her, "chances are it wasn't counterfeit, or you'd know by now."

"Oh." She blinked at him. "Well, that's something, anyway." And she leaned back, sighing. "But how am I going to tell her? Poor Mama, she was so proud of him. Thought he was all set. Doing well, making money, maybe ready to settle—*I* should've known," she added bitterly, "when I saw that snapshot. He sent it in his card. Merry Christmas from your hippie son." She smiled humorlessly. "Long hair, beard, the whole silly get-up. Sitting on this motorcycle with some girl up behind him like he thought he owned the world. I brought it with me in case—"

Digging in her cheap plastic handbag, she produced the snapshot, which she handed to Krug. He looked at it silently, then passed it over to Casey. A candid color shot, obviously taken with a good camera, for it was clear enough that both subjects were easily identifiable. The man was Gerald Barrett. The girl was unmistakably Susannah Roche.

NINETEEN

"Didn't I tell you, Al?" Harry Berger kept crowing abrasively—a Moshe Dayan-style diplomat, Casey thought, lumps first, soft talk later. "*Didn't* I? Okay, you got her wired to Barrett now. And she was Johnny-on-the-spot when they took him out. No way to figure it but she was going with him, right?"

"Some cool pussycat if she was," Krug came back at him. "She's half a block away. Couple minutes closer and they'd of had her, too. But she shows up as a witness calm as can be? Even you and your Treasury buddies ought to be able to figure that one out."

"Bait makes better sense, Harry," Casey said reasonably. "If she was planning to run with Barrett, the last thing she'd do is expose herself—"

But Berger wasn't listening; he had news too, it seemed. "Turns out Barrett bought the Mercedes last December. Had no credit rating, the dealer told me. But his down payment was big enough they let him have it on a contract with a balloon payment in six months." He scowled at Krug. "That's now, *bubi*. Score time for everybody. What it looks like is that Barrett held out on his partners and boosted the purchase price of the counterfeiting equipment so he could buy himself a flashy car. That's why he kept it stashed, see? A little advance bonus he gave himself, the dumb schmuck."

The feds had been busy too, he went on. Taking Barrett's pad as their center, an army of agents had been out beating the bushes, checking every printing shop listed in both telephone and business directories in areas of five, then ten, then twenty miles from Barrett's apartment. "Idea is, even a dude like him probably wouldn't want to hit the freeway everyday," he said, shrugging. "Good enough guess, I just hope they're right."

Anything unlikely or suspicious was being checked, he told them. Closures of print shops due to sickness or vacation—which, in this season, made the job that much harder. Any unusual activity noticed by neighbors. Anything out of the usual run of business.

"Got enough already to keep 'em busy for two months," he sighed. "Not only firm names, proprietor names, too. And you figure the time we've got"—Berger made a throwaway gesture— "like none left! They'll have the goods moved and peddled to some mob before anybody's ass is even near the sling."

The squad's preliminary investigation had already been assembled, Casey discovered when Berger finally left—the sort of shoe-leather report which is standard in all cases of violent death. Subject's physician, lawyer, landlord had been covered; names listed in a personal telephone directory were checked out; Teletype queries were already following up on the few letters which had been discovered on the premises of the deceased. Susannah Roche apparently had no family, at least none detectives had been able to locate so far. She owned a red Porsche, which was parked in the subterranean garage of the apartment building. Like Barrett, she appeared to have plenty of money, but no bank accounts. Rent had been paid in cash each month, and there was no evidence of any charge accounts. As references on her rental agreement, she had listed an actors' agent and a professional photographer.

"Both dead ends," Lieutenant Timms said disgustedly. "The agent claims she hasn't worked for over a year, and since December he hasn't even heard from her. Photographer's even dimmer. Claims she's no friend at all, he only knows her from one session of shooting publicity stills a couple years ago."

"Looks like December was connection time for everybody. Maybe Rees, too?" Krug rubbed his hands. "Better shoot word off to Frisco—get a line on who he buddied with in the slammer."

"That's reaching for it, Al," Timms objected. "We've got an eyewitness now says she went home alone." It was the delivery-man for the *Los Angeles Times*, he said. There were twenty sub-scribers to the morning metropolitan newspaper in Susannah Roche's building—which put the deliveryman inside about ten or fifteen minutes. "Claims he got there before five o'clock, and he was just pulling away when he spotted a woman wearing a big hat going in. The description sounds right, and he's positive she was alone—so that probably lets Rees out."

"The hell it does," Krug muttered.

But Timms ignored him. "What we can assume from what we've got here..." He was shuffling through the reports on his desk. "Time, the way she was dressed, et cetera, she walked in and it happened immediately—whatever it was. The woman in 1006 heard somebody enter the Roche apartment around three. Two hours later, after the screaming, the neighbor in 1004—that's the stockbroker—thinks he might've heard somebody running down the hall. The stairway's at the opposite end from the eleva-tor, which'd take anybody using it by 1004, so it could be kosher."

"And the so-called security guard was probably snoozing," Krug said sourly. "So, for the second time in two days, our ama-teur hit man was home free."

"If there was a hit man."

"Took a souvenir with him, too, maybe." Casey consciously misread his partner's scowl. "If she was strong-armed, that hat she was wearing would've been knocked off. And if it didn't go out the window, where is it?"

"Ah, for Chrissake," Krug snarled, "quit playing Sherlock. There's sixteen different hats in her closet!"

"But no black straw one trimmed with sequins, Al."

"My partner, the fashion expert."

"All right," Timms said impatiently, "let's not hassle the details. We've got enough to sweat about already. What'd you do with the sister?"

"Checked her into the Miramar," Krug said. "I'll pick her up at nine-thirty tomorrow for the inquest."

Timms kept rubbing his forehead, staring at the snapshot which was lying on his desk. "You're sure this couldn't be a look-alike, Al."

"No way."

"Couldn't miss that smile, sir," Casey agreed.

Timms sighed gustily. "All right, get copies run off right away. I want her apartment house covered from top to bottom again." Haynes and Zwingler drew a repeat of their previous assignment also—another shoe-leather canvass of every house backing onto the alley where Barrett had been killed, from Montana Avenue to Alta. When this was completed, they were to cover Alta again, all this in hopes of finding someone who might have spotted a red Porsche parked near the alley, or possibly a woman on foot—not a hopeful task considering that the time in question was four in the morning. "Al, you and Kellog hit that restaurant and those people who gave that party she took Rees to last night. Sit on that motel if you have to, and when he shows again, take him with you to locate the place. And when you do, pry a guest list out of them right away so we can get to work on it. What we're looking for now is the next connection."

After a twenty-minute scenic drive up the Coast Highway, they ran into a nasty traffic snarl. One northbound lane was closed off, and a pair of motorcycle officers stood by, directing the stream of backed-up traffic. Pulling up beside the nearest one, Casey flashed his badge. "What's going on?"

"Slide up ahead. You fellas want an escort?"

"No thanks, we'll manage on our own."

"Whatever you say." The young face under the black-and-white helmet beamed in through the window at them, glossy with happy self-importance. He tossed a breezy salute. "Good hunting!" Then he strutted off, his boots gleaming in the late sunlight.

"Look at that kook," Krug grunted. " 'Good hunting,' for Chrissake. Assholes all act like forties flyboys."

Up ahead now, they could see road crews and heavy equipment scooping at the wide tail of decomposed granite which had slid down over the pavement—one of the natural hazards of the area. The towering palisades that walled the land side of this highway had been crumbling for as long as Casey could remember, but so far there had never been a fatality, only some near misses. Another everyday miracle which local residents took for granted.

Directly across the highway from the slide, he could see the restaurant sign—Ultimate Perception—and cutting between slow-moving southbound cars, Casey swung into the graveled parking lot. The place was closed, as they had expected, but it surprised them when there was no answer to their pounding on the door. A janitor might have left already, but kitchen staff for a dinnerhouse should be at work by this time.

Krug tried the long gates in a fence connected to the south side of the building, but they were closed tight. Over the tall, solid board fencing, Casey spied what looked like the top part of a tarpaulin-covered shed inside. Or maybe a load of building materials—

"Get the emergency number," Krug was saying. "Got to be posted on the door somewhere."

It was, and from a public phone in a gas station down the highway, Casey tried the number. But there was no answer.

"Try the Sheriff's station," Krug advised. "Could be the owner lives in town." Meaning Los Angeles. "Somebody there'll know."

"Sure, we got a number here," the desk man at the Malibu station of the Los Angeles County Sheriff's Department told Casey. He sounded young and bored and inclined to gossip if given half a chance—a country policeman. "Licensee of record is Victor Russo, but his son really owns the joint. Rodman. Had a couple vice busts years ago up north someplace, so he couldn't make it with the Board of Equalization. Had to get his old man to front for him on the liquor license." He reeled off the telephone number Casey already had. "Anything going on there we ought to know about?"

"No, just a routine inquiry. You happen to know any names of anybody who works there—like a waiter, maybe?"

"You got to be—Hey, wait a minute. Come to think of it, one of the girls here…" His voice faded away and distantly Casey heard him calling to someone named Hetty or Letty. Then there was a long wait while they gabbled, their voices incomprehensible, mixed with the clack of typewriters, phones ringing, office racket. Startlingly loud, someone breathed in his ear, saying, softly, "Yeah. Okay, love-face, I'll get back to *you* later. You still there, Santa Monica?"

"Still here, love-face."

The deputy laughed. "You weren't supposed to hear that. Okay, a clerk here in the office has this brother works there part time. You want to talk to him, I got the address and phone number…"

Since they would be passing the waiter's home on their way back to Santa Monica—the address was approximately two miles south of there—Casey didn't bother calling first. Krug whistled appreciatively as they pulled up before what looked to be a modern and expensive condominium on the beach side of the highway ten minutes later. "Pretty fancy for a waiter. Hustling tables must be good these days."

A gray-haired, rather pretty woman wearing a wildly patterned muumuu answered the door. That they were policemen did not seem to bother her at all. "Charley's having a swim," she told them cheerfully. "But he won't be long. Says the water freezes his you-know-whats. Just have a seat, and I'll pour you—"

"No, thanks, ma'am," Krug refused hastily. "We'll just leave a card. Your son can call us when he—"

"Oh no you don't," she cried gaily. "You're not getting away from here without telling me what this's about. *He* won't, that's for sure!" The idea seemed to amuse her. "Now you just sit down over there and tell Mama everything."

"Ma'am, we're short of time—"

"Now, you stop that!" She waggled an admonishing finger under Krug's nose. "You be nice or I'll write one of my nasty letters, and *then* you'll be sorry!"

Greek meets Greek, Casey kept thinking as they chose chairs and she served them coffee after they refused beer. Krug's wife was perhaps one of these steam-roller ladies? Part-extortionist, part-flirt; Circes, Cassandras, and sometimes, sadly, Medeas—

"Well, no wonder you didn't find anybody there," she was saying in answer to Krug's inquiry about the restaurant. "They're probably running all over town trying to find a range."

"A range, ma'am?"

"Stove. You know. Can't cook on just anything at a restaurant. You've got to have professional equipment…"

Someone she called Freddy had phoned early this afternoon, she told them, informing Charley, her son, that the stove had blown up; they'd be forced to close down the dining part of the restaurant this evening. Charley had been terribly disappointed, of course. He simply loved his work there. So many interesting people. And all so witty. Charley said it was Freddy who drew the crowd. A lot of show-business people—

"That's very interesting," Casey interrupted—acting as safety valve, since Krug looked ready to explode. "But what we're really inquiring about is a couple that had dinner there last night. A routine matter." He stood up. "So if you'll have your son call—"

"Isn't he nervous," she said to Krug. "Something about your work, I suppose? Anyway," she went on cozily, "about Freddy. He's just been wonderful to my boy. *So* kind. You wouldn't think it to look at him, either. Such a—well, you know how they can be. Snippy sometimes. Nasty. But not Freddy. I've got some pictures here—they're in Charley's room. He gave them to Charley a while ago. Simply gorgeous things! You wouldn't guess in a million years it was a man. He used to perform in San Francisco. As a—what d'you call it when they dress up like women? Anyway, his wardrobe alone cost him thousands, he told Charley."

"*Women*," Krug groaned when they had finally escaped. "A fag son with pinups of some drag queen in his room—and what's her reaction? *She* drools over 'em, too!"

"You think that restaurant's a homosexual hangout, Al?"

"Got to be."

Casey started the Mustang. "Why do you suppose Rees took her to a place like that?"

"Maybe *she* took him." Krug sucked in his breath as they gunned into the southbound coastal traffic which was fast-moving now. "Christ, I keep riding with you, for sure I'll never live to collect my pension! What's the big rush?"

"Heavy evening, Al. I've got to check out in an hour, or I'm in trouble."

"Better get on the phone, then," Krug advised callously. "We got a lot of territory to cover yet."

Casey's heart sank. Good old Uncle Al, mentor and tormentor. Knowing from experience that argument would be useless, he tried suggestion instead: "After we check Rees again, that's it, isn't it, Al? Nothing left to cover that night tour can't handle."

But Krug only grunted. His mind was obviously elsewhere. "Before we hit Rees, let's swing by and pick up his suitcases from the lab. Try it roundabout this time." Now he was smiling, Casey noticed. Your friendly neighborhood bloodhound. "Even the smartest crook's got to fumble it sooner or later—right, sport? They all do. So maybe this is the time for Rees, hah?"

TWENTY

In his shallow sleep, he heard the car pulling into the court-yard, and the dream he had dreamed almost continuously in prison started unreeling again: rain falling, and his headlights picking out quicksilver drops; Ellen beside him with the letter in her hand, smiling, pointing across the street at a mailbox. *No, don't bother to turn around, I'll just run across—*

Car doors slammed, echoing the same sound in his dream, and he jerked awake, the cold sweat of apprehension like grease on his skin. *I'll just run across.* He could still hear her footsteps. Then he realized these were real ones, scrape-scraping across the asphalt paving. Coming here? Rees looked for the time, saw he had slept away the afternoon. It was almost five.

The knocking on his door was surprisingly quiet. Maybe not Krug after all? But no one else would be coming here—

"Mr. Rees?"

His heart clenched. "Just a minute." The plastic bag containing pieces of the shoe-box lid was still sitting on the floor of his car.

"About those suitcases," Krug said by way of greeting. "Seems like your snoop didn't leave any prints, Mr. Rees. Thought we'd check back, see if you had any ideas."

Rees looked from one to the other, trying to fathom their purpose. "You've impounded my bags?"

"Nah, they're in the car. You want to get 'em, Casey?"

The younger one nodded. "Only take a second." He headed for the Mustang, which was parked near Rees's door.

"You look hot," Krug commented. "Been exercising, Mr. Rees?"

"No, I was asleep."

"Bad dreams, hah?"

"Is that an official question, Sergeant?"

Krug's eyes froze. "Don't push it—"

"Here we are. Excuse me, Mr. Rees." Casey set the two bags just inside the door, resting the shaving kit on top of them. Then they both stepped in without invitation, and Krug closed the door—another question-and-answer session, Rees realized. Subject, the money again. Where had it really come from? Why was he carrying so much? According to their report from San Francisco—

"For God's sake," he groaned, "I'm not a criminal! Don't you know that by now? If you don't, you should."

"Then you won't mind telling us where you got it, right?"

"Wrong, Sergeant, it's none of your business." Had the young one spotted the plastic bag in his car? Not enough time to inspect it, though. And if he didn't antagonize them—"All right," he said, "I won it gambling. In a—a poker game." He slumped onto the foot of the bed. On one beefy haunch, Krug perched on the corner of a combination desk and dressing table with a mirror hanging over it. Casey took the only chair, which sat in a corner. He had his notebook out. "Fresno, I think it was," Rees elaborated, realizing as he spoke that he should have waited for them to ask. "I met some salesmen in a bar and we got together later."

"Like in a motel, maybe?"

"Yes. But I can't remember the name." He swallowed cottony dryness, despising himself for his lies, his fear of them, the unmanning sense of being their victim. The motel was a newish place on the highway, he told them. No, he didn't remember any names of the men he had played with, or mention of companies they had worked for—

"Well, maybe you'll think of them later," Casey said sooth-ingly. "Incidentally, we've run across a little discrepancy, Mr. Rees. Just a detail about how you said Miss Roche was dressed. Haven't been able to locate that black hat—"

"I don't know anything," Rees began violently, then stopped himself. "She picked it up at the party, that's all I know. If you'll check with the Godwins—"

"Who?" Krug said.

Casey consulted his notebook. "This morning you said the name was Jervis."

"It's on their postbox. E and J Godwin. J for Jervis. I sup-pose," he added lamely.

There was a short silence then, terrifying to Rees because it was obvious they weren't through with him yet. Casey finally asked how long he had stayed in Fresno, and he thought, God, back to that again. Just the one night, he answered, then it was Krug's turn again. How many hours would Rees guess it had taken him to drive the distance from Frisco to Fresno? Recognizing a trick question, he realized they must know when he had left San Francisco, so he answered simply—the truth this time—he had not driven straight through. No, he couldn't name exactly where he had stopped. Near Monterey one night. An inland town near the mountain another night—

"You got a short memory," Krug cut him off. "But maybe it'll get better about the last couple of days?" Holding one knee, he rocked himself backward, banging the mirror slightly, and their images in it shimmered, distorting like water reflections. "This date you had last night, for instance. What'd you talk about, Mr. Rees? All those hours you must've rapped about something besides the weather. Like her career, maybe?" His tone made it a joke. "Or the story of your life? Or something like your impres-sions of the slammer? Or maybe what a lousy place this is com-pared to sophisticated San Francisco?"

Rees gritted his teeth. Bastard. Bullyboy. "I'm afraid I don't recall anything specific, Sergeant. As you said, it was a long evening."

"Yeah, but you had something in common. Stands to reason—"

"If you mean the hit-and-run, Miss Roche didn't want to discuss it."

"Yeah, I bet Miss Roche didn't." His smile was mean. "Too nasty to bring up while you're having yourselves such a nice time, hah? She happened to mention how long she'd known Barrett?"

Rees stared at him, speechless.

"The guy on the motorcycle, remember? Gerald Hower Barrett. Turns out he was her boyfriend."

"You're crazy—she no more knew him than I did!"

"Well, that's another question, isn't it?" Krug was still smiling. "The sixty-four-dollar one, right, Mr. Rees? And you can bet your bottom dollar, we'll have the answer—and soon."

TWENTY-ONE

They kept asking questions, which he answered without calculation, sheathed now in shock, numbness, incomprehension. And when they walked out finally, leaving him slumped on the foot of the bed, Rees could not recall what else had been said. He listened to the Mustang start up and pull slowly out of the asphalt-paved motel courtyard. Petty worries kept surfacing in his consciousness: he must settle his room rent for the night; it was long past the posted checkout time. Sometime this evening he should investigate the complicated downtown Los Angeles freeway system because he had no idea how to reach the Parole Authority. His appointment was for nine sharp tomorrow morning.

Krug's grin seemed printed on the stale joyless dusk in his room. *She tell you how long she'd known Barrett?* He groaned aloud. *Turns out he was her boyfriend.* Nausea coiling like a serpent in him, he saw her clearly: Susannah laughing. *Play it for giggles.* Susannah giggling. *Ooo-wow-you-scare-me.* Susannah clamped to him like a fiery limpet. *What you can't see can only kill you.*

But the fact of her death was far away now.

He showered quickly, shaved and dressed in fresh clothing. The evening air outside was cool, he found, smelling of the sea and sprinkled lawns in the park across the way. By the door of the motel office, three newspaper-vending machines were chained to the wall, and headlines inside one caught his eye: ACTRESS

PLUNGES TO DEATH. The newspaper was local—the *Evening Outlook*—and as he inserted a dime in the slot, opening the lid of the vendor, Rees saw a subheading in smaller caps which stated that the deceased had figured as a witness in another death.

Her boyfriend's.

A spasm like laughter choking him, he pushed open the Plexiglas door of the motel office, and eyes watering, smiled stiffly at the woman standing behind the desk counter. "I'm in Number Eleven. Almost forgot to pay you for tonight."

"Oh, yes. Mr. Rees." Her expression was faintly disapproving. "That trouble you had this morning all straightened out now?"

The irony was unintentional, he knew, but the knowledge did not allay the bitterness seething in him.

"Let's see, that's fourteen-fifty. Out of twenty?"

Boyfriend, he kept thinking while she handed him the change. *Boyfriend.* She said something about his car which he missed in his abstraction, and oblivious to her pleasant comment to have a nice evening, he walked out again, the rolled newspaper like a club in his hand.

After leaving the Pelican Motel, they had dropped down off the palisades by way of a steep street locally called the California Incline. And on the Coast Highway shortly afterward, they had located the mailbox Rees had described: *E & J Godwin.* Casey parked as near as he was able in the congested area, and they walked back to the house—another waste of time, as they soon discovered, for the Godwins were either not at home or not answering.

"Could be they're out on the beach," Krug said. "Let's try the neighbors, maybe they can spot 'em for us."

There was no answer at the adjacent house north. But at the weathered shingle-sided bungalow to the south, a boy about ten wearing a Mickey Mouse beanie opened the door. A round ill-defined Jack o' lantern face. Krug sighed audibly. No mistaking that the boy was retarded. "We're looking for the people next door," he said slowly and distinctly. "The Godwins? Thought maybe you might've seen 'em on the beach this evening."

The boy shook his head.

"You know what they look like?" Casey asked, getting a grimace for reply. "Maybe your mother does," he suggested. "You want to tell her—?"

"Bobby, who is it?" A worn-looking homely woman wearing a terrycloth robe peered out at them. "Oh, police," she sighed when Casey identified himself, repeating that they'd been trying to reach her neighbors—a routine matter, but they needed to talk to them. "Listen, the only thing *I* know is they're a menace. I mean, people their age trying to be swingers, it's ridiculous! And that house, you should see it inside. Like a regular freak show! And those parties, my God, they never—" She stopped abruptly. "Listen, if it's about what goes on there, I don't want to be involved. I mean, we moved here thinking it'd be good for Bobby to run on the beach. Never had any idea we'd be living next to—"

"When was the last time you saw them?" Krug interrupted.

"This morning. After their stupid party finally broke up."

"What time was this?"

"Well, early." She ran a nervous hand through her brittle-looking, badly bleached hair. "About seven, maybe. I was getting breakfast, and I could see her over there cleaning up the patio. Probably hadn't even been to bed yet. Parading around in that orange caftan that makes her look like a pregnant cow. And they were fighting. She kept yelling at him—"

"But you didn't see them leave?"

"Listen, I'm not that interested! Anyway, we've been gone most of the day. Took Bobby to Disneyland—"

They got her name, which was Killigrew. She spelled it carefully, then warned them again that she didn't intend to be involved in any trouble. Anyway, she knew nothing about the Godwins. One look at that house had been enough to convince her that even ordinary neighborliness would be out of the question.

"Love thy whatchamacallit," Krug muttered when she had slammed the door. "Looks like Rees's party story was kosher. So why was he so cute about the name this morning?" He blew out his breath. "Ah, the hell with it, let's leave a note for the swingers. If that don't work, we'll get Smitty to keep calling 'em till he raises somebody."

Whatever the police knew they were keeping it to themselves. Rees wadded up the newsprint he had read and reread until he had almost memorized it, pitching it across the room. *What you can't see*, her voice kept chanting in his mind. Her smile, shimmering like fox-fire, revealed shapeless shadows in the swamp of his memory: fleeting impressions which had a plaguing, frightening mysteriousness now. He had been used last night for some purpose unknown to him.

If only he knew *why*, Rees thought wildly. Something about the hat? But perhaps checking how she was dressed was only police routine. So is hassling me. An ex-con, after all.

Krug's mean man's grin burned behind his eyes. That's another question, isn't it? Feeling the ache of pressure mounting in him, Rees tried to relax, stretching, shuddering as he yawned and yawned like a nervous animal. Susannah and Barrett. What in God's name was he involved in? Barrett and Susannah. The detectives would head now for the beach house. But people like the Godwins won't welcome police.

But they'll talk to me, he thought as he left the motel. They have to now.

Over the sea, a saffron glow suffused the horizon; gulls flying northward looked black as cinders against it. Lights were already burning on the pier, Rees noticed, pale bluish pinpricks in the sunset flame, which was fading fast as he turned his Volkswagen off Ocean onto a sloping street which gave access to the Coast Highway. Aware of the possibility that the detectives might still be there, he drove by the Godwins' house first, scrutinizing all the cars parked at the curb nearby. But there was no Mustang to be seen. At a public parking lot several doors south, he pulled in and swung around in order to avoid making a U-turn on the highway. Traffic north and south was heavy, and unsure that he would be able to cross it a second time in order to park in front of the house, he decided to leave the Volks there and walk back.

All the houses in this section—Rees counted six as he passed by—were of the same vintage as the Godwins'. All old frames probably built in the early twenties. Weekend cottages on narrow lots which soaring land values had priced into the class of desirable full-time residences. There was something stuck in the Godwins' door, he saw—a business card printed *Santa Monica Police Department*, with Krug's name in small letters at the bottom. On the back someone had scrawled: *For informational purposes only, please call as soon as possible.*

Without much hope of reply, Rees knocked loudly. But what he was counting on now was a more private entrance—the beachside patio, the French doors which had been open last night. He'd have to walk back to the parking lot, he realized, since there was no public access to the beach until then. Better count houses again to make sure, he told himself as he stuck Krug's card back into the crack between the front door and its weathered frame. Wouldn't do at this point to trespass by mistake in the wrong patio.

He was starting back, retracing his steps, when he noticed the narrow garage door at the south side of the house. Unlike their neighbors, the Godwins had not remodeled, adding the garage to their living space. Rees hesitated again. If a car's in there, chances are they're home. So look, he told himself. Nobody's going to arrest you for taking a look in a garage.

The door was cumbersome, cross-braced like a shed door and difficult to move. But when Rees cracked it open, a slight breeze caught the door, swinging it wide, throwing him off balance. Inside stood an old two-door Renault, once white, but now rusty from the sea air. Through the rear window, he could see what looked like luggage stacked in the back seat.

Without considering the risk or his right to do so, Rees stepped into the garage and opened the car door on the driver's side. The load in the back seat was luggage, all right—packed full, he discovered when he hefted one bag. In the corner of the back seat nearest him, someone had wadded a poplin trench coat. A man's raincoat. The sleeve he could see was partly rolled up, exposing the faded yellow-and-black tartan lining.

Rees yanked the coat out of the car. The other sleeve was rolled up also, and this one had a peculiar wedge-shaped tear in the lining. It was the coat Susannah had been wearing the first time he had seen her—in the alley where the motorcyclist had died.

TWENTY-TWO

As soon as they checked into the squad room again, Casey dialed Tinytown Toys. There was no answer from the switchboard, and with a wild feeling that he had lost her already, he tried Joey's home number which rang and rang, hollow and shrill in his ear, bell pealing endlessly in a deserted house.

"No answer, hah?" Krug had flopped at his desk and was busily scribbling something. "Better luck next time, sport."

"She's probably on her way home, got held up in traffic."

"Sure—or maybe she's a mind reader. Five'll get you ten she's already fixed up with another guy."

"Very funny." Casey peered over his partner's shoulder. "What's this?" It was a query, he saw, to be directed north, asking for information about Paul Rees's friendships and contacts in prison. "Al, what's the point of this? You're trying to have it both ways, don't you see that? Rees can't be part of the counterfeit setup and a key witness, too."

"Don't bet on it, genius, you could lose your shirt. Ah come on," Krug added impatiently, "quit worrying about the facts and take a look at all those so-called coincidences. Like that five hundred bucks that turned into a couple, three thousand, maybe more. Or that one-day trip he claims took him four to make. Or just happening to be a witness at four A.M., and then connecting all of a sudden with Witness Number Two—*who* just also happens to turn out to be the victim's chick."

"And maybe Victim Number Two. Okay," Casey admitted, "it's a load of something—" but one of the outside lines was buzzing and he lost his audience.

"Detective Bureau," Krug barked into the receiver. "Sergeant—Oh, hi, Denny, what's up?"

Casey could hear the quacking at the other end—Haynes with something hot, obviously.

"The suspense is killing me," Krug was saying with heavy sarcasm. "What's so big you can't—Okay, we'll wait, we'll *wait*." He slammed the receiver. "Showboats. That was Denny. Says hold everything, they've got a bombshell. Be in right away."

While they waited for Haynes and Zwingler to check in, Casey made a fast trip to the lab downstairs.

"Got some reports ready, if you're interested," McGregor told him. He grinned at Casey's sigh of relief. "Pressure getting to you, young fella? I hear Al's really hipped on nailing that ex-con." But diplomatically, he didn't wait for agreement or denial. "You've got word on the Mercedes already. Blurring on the steering wheel—probably gloves, anyway no prints. Specks of some shiny stuff in the back seat. Too soon for analysis yet. Grit on the floor's the usual combination, but we're sorting it out in case anybody's interested." In the Roche apartment, he went on, they had managed to gather at least six different sets of prints, almost all clear enough for identification—*if* they were on file. "Got some word here on the vacuum job, too." He pawed through the papers stacked on his desk. "Here it is. Some hairs on the pillows that don't match hers. Also some stuff we got out of that fake-fur bedspread. Carpet fluff mostly, and a few grains of what looks like crushed rock. Saliva analysis from those cigar butts in her bedroom is ready, too."

"Any of those prints match the ones you lifted out of the Mercedes?"

"Well, a couple could be Barrett's, but they're only fragments."

"How about Rees?"

"Some possibles, but nothing clear enough to stand up in court. A couple on the front doorknob is all. Looks like you'll have to hang something else on him."

Casey intended trying Joey's number again when he returned upstairs. But when he walked into the squad room, he found that Haynes and Zwingler had just arrived, both wearily self-congratulative over finding one of their previously checked not-at-homes finally home at last.

"Citizen named Kingsley," Zwingler was saying happily. "He and his wife live a couple houses from the corner of Fourteenth on the north side of Alta. They went up to Santa Maria yesterday to visit their son, but the missus got sick—"

"For Chrissake," Krug snarled, "skip the social notes."

"Okay, they woke up about four yesterday morning, see. Figured they might as well get up and get an early start driving north. Their bedroom's at the front of the house, and they sleep with the shades up—you get the picture?—so they don't turn a light on right away. Missus is getting into her robe and slippers, and he's standing there in his pajamas starting to pull down the shades when he sees this car come belting out of the alley down the street. A Mercedes, he's sure of it. While he's watching, it pulls up, and he sees this girl jump out of the back seat—"

"He get a good look at her?" Casey interrupted.

"Right near the streetlight. That good enough? A young dame in some kind of a crazy outfit, Kingsley said. And this big hat with sparkle stuff on it."

"Congratulations," Casey said. "There's our missing—"

But Zwingler wasn't stopping for any further comment. "She jumps out of the back seat, Kingsley claims. Takes the hat off, and tosses it in the car. Then she throws on this raincoat the driver hands out to her. *Then* she heads back for the alley, and the car takes off again like a bat out of hell. Somebody's wife was what

Kingsley figured. Getting dumped quick by her boyfriend before her husband spotted them. Anyhow, all it took was about a minute or less, he told me."

"And an hour later, she's sitting here signing a witness statement." Casey sighed, remembering the ravishing smile. "She had a lot of guts."

"That's for sure. And you can see what happened," Haynes said soggily, mopping his nose. "They spot they've got a witness, so she jumps out to get a line on how much he saw—"

"*Bull*shit," Krug exploded. "Don't give me that 'line' baloney! She's sitting there in the back seat with some big hat on. Got shiny stuff all over it. No missing it if you got any kind of a look—but our star witness never mentions a word."

"Well, an alley," Haynes said doubtfully. "At four in the morning, it's got to be pitch black there."

"But not so black he can't spot the car as a Mercedes."

"Yeah, and a black one at that." Zwingler nodded. "You got something there, Al."

"The car would have passed by the laundromat windows," Casey reminded them. "And don't forget, his wife went the same way. Rees was probably in shock when we talked to him."

"*Every* time?" Krug hooted.

"Maybe he did spot her," Haynes suggested. "Maybe laid it on her last night she better pay off?"

"Now you're talking," Krug said. "For sure they had some kind of a ploy going, but that smart hooker outsmarted herself."

Timms came in then, interrupting their discussion, and Zwingler repeated the story. "So maybe it's the next connection?" The lieutenant looked pleased, but cautiously so. "If Rees's story that she picked up the hat at the party is straight, could be the Godwins or one of their guests—"

"Yeah, or a foul ball," Krug growled. "With our ex-con's average so far, I'd lay money on it." But he was already in motion, unconsciously checking the Detective Special in its belt holster under his shabby sports jacket. "Anybody buying steak if we don't strike out?"

Casey caught up with him on the stairs. "No takers, Al."

"Bunch of pikers," Krug grunted. "Won't even bet on a sure thing."

TWENTY-THREE

His skin felt tight, his body swollen, the fingers clamping the raincoat as thick as sausages. Sand filled his shoes, gritted in his socks, but Rees was unaware of it tramping up the beach, for the whole of his being was focused like a burning glass on confronting Jervis Godwin.

The patio of the house next door to the Godwins' was lighted, he noticed vaguely. A boy wearing a Mickey Mouse hat was bouncing a ball, missing every time, running awkwardly to retrieve it. He stopped to stare as Rees crossed the sandy lot to the Godwins' unlighted beachside patio. Ignoring him, Rees peered through the French doors into a dark room he couldn't quite remember.

Shapes of chairs and a long couch made indistinct shadows, tantalizing, enraging. No crack of light from any direction showed inside the house. Lying low, Rees thought savagely. By full dark they would have been on their way in the loaded Renault, carrying all the answers with them. "Godwin," he shouted, pounding on the French door frame with the flat of his hand. "I know you're in there!"

No reply. No trace of movement. Still no light showing anywhere inside. The idea of a trap of some kind flitted through Rees's mind as he tried the knob, feeling it turn easily. Both halves of the glass-paned door swung open slightly. Pushing them wider, he stepped two paces into the room, then stopped again, calling, "Godwin, I'm not leaving here till I talk to you!" hearing his own voice die away in the musty dusk which, deeper into the room, became impenetrable darkness.

God *damn*, where was a light? He moved forward, tripped over something—a coffee table—and overbalanced, fell half on, half off the long couch. Using the cushions to steady himself, he straightened again, still clutching the coat. He spied a glimmer of metal—a standing lamp at the other end of the couch. Fumbling for the switch to turn it on, Rees was aware of his own loud, rapid breathing. His fingers found a knob and turned it. And as light burst like a soundless explosion in the room, his breath whistled out of him.

Godwin was sitting in the far corner. Sitting still in a chair, his head tilted to one side mockingly, eyes glistening. His mouth was open as if he meant to laugh or scream, but no sound came forth.

"Oh my *God*," Rees whispered, moving slowly closer.

The left side of Godwin's head resting so coyly on his left shoulder looked half eaten away. Blasted away. And that whole side of his body was a sticky mass of drying blood. He had been shot point-blank in the right ear, Rees's horror-struck perceptions noted; even to his untrained eye, the powder burns were apparent.

Another suicide, his mind registered numbly. But even as he thought this, his searching eyes fed back the message of no gun in sight. "Wife," he whispered. Emma. Emily. Could she—?

But through the open door into what had been built as a dining room, he saw a paler-than-darkness bundle heaped on the floor. A human bundle.

Just inside was a light switch found blindly by instinct. He flicked it on, saw the woman's blank chalky face, the pool of blood, and flicked it off again, standing panting in a dark now whirling with retinal ghosts. All the ordinary impulses— phone for ambulance, phone for police, run yelling for help to neighbors—leaped to life in him and died instantly, killed by a piercing vision of Krug.

Then somewhere in the dark house a phone began ringing. And dropping the coat, Rees bolted.

TWENTY-FOUR

"Less than half an hour ago. Maybe only fifteen minutes. Bobby saw him. He went in through the patio door—same as you did—and he was yelling, Bobby said."

"Yelling what, Mrs. Killigrew?"

"Well, I don't suppose Bobby could hear exactly. I mean, with the surf and all. Anyway, he was only in there a few minutes, Bobby said. Then he came running out"—she pointed south—"that way. Isn't that right, Bobby?" She tweaked the boy's hat. "Honey, isn't that what you told Mama?" But he only looked at her blankly.

Well, it was almost dark, after all, she went on defensively when they asked her to try to get a description from her son. And Bobby had been playing in the light. Probably all he'd been able to see was a shadow. Anyway, a child his age. Well, he couldn't be expected to notice the same things as an adult, could he?

The information they were finally able to extract was virtually useless for purposes of identification—a person, probably a man, in darkish clothing; probably hatless; who might or might not be of medium height.

"Boy, we really got it all going for us in the witness department," Krug kept grousing while they plodded through the sand back to the Godwin house. "Ain't we the lucky Sherlocks? A one-time loser as phony as they come, and a dummy can't even talk so you can understand him."

"Well, as long as his mother can translate—"

"So what's that mean? A lot of secondhand crap, that's all. What she's interested in is making her kid look good."

By now the inevitable cluster of onlookers had gathered on the beach near the Godwins' patio, watching the four patrolmen with extra-power flashlights who were searching the area for the weapon. They found out later that a fifth member of the team had been sent out to round up metal detectors of the sort beach-combers used—a useless task, as was the search, it turned out, because the murder gun was not in the vicinity.

Without apology, Krug shoved through the rubbernecks, and following him, Casey tried to guess when he might be able to phone again. Too late now anyway, he thought gloomily. She had been sitting there for hours—no dinner, no excuses, stood up. In her book the name Kellog would be writ in mud now. Mud, or worse. They never told you at the Academy that police work in the detectives grades would doom you to a life totally devoid of anything as human as romance.

When they entered the beach house again, a flash bulb popped, its phosphorescent glare taking color from the faces of the technicians. Lieutenant Timms had arrived, Casey saw. Krug buttonholed him immediately, covering the question of their entry as an emergency procedure: they had knocked on the front door, and not getting any answer, had hoofed it down the road till they could get through to the beach. "When we got here it was open"—Krug pointed to the French doors—"and that lamp was on. Spotted him right away. Took a couple minutes before we found out we had a double bill going here."

"Not quite, Al." Timms was smiling slightly. "Turns out the woman's alive. She's on her way to the hospital."

"For Chrissake, after three hits and all that blood lost?"

"Could be a real break, Al."

"Don't count your chickens, Lieutenant," the medical man working over the corpse in the corner advised. "With the injuries she sustained, they'll be lucky to get her into surgery still alive."

"You got any ideas about time yet?" Krug asked him.

"Three, four hours ago, maybe. Tell you better after the coagulation tests."

"That lets out our mysterious assailant." Krug explained Mrs. Killigrew's story to the lieutenant. "Looks like the kid's either stringing us along, or somebody beat us to the punch here."

"Could be." Timms nodded. "There's a coat on the floor there. Looks like somebody dropped it. Maybe it was your visitor."

Pulling one of the lab's portable high-intensity lamps closer, they crouched near the raincoat. Without shifting its position on the floor, Timms flipped back one lapel. "No maker's label." He reached delicately into a pocket, pulling out a matchbook bearing the imprint *Mayfair Markets,* a huge grocery chain. "Not much help there, either."

"Sleeves rolled up," Krug muttered. "A ratty old raincoat with a plaid lining?"

Casey nodded. "Could be the same one she was wearing, Al. Which means Rees can probably identify it."

Krug pushed himself upright, his knee joints cracking. "Let's get the pictures and tagging done pronto. If we can get a make on this coat, for sure it pegs Godwin as Barrett's killer."

"Unless the killer dropped it here accidentally, or on purpose." Timms sucked his teeth. "Before you do anything else, hit the kid next door again. See if you can get anything more about how the guy he saw was dressed. Or if he was carrying a coat. And this time, Al," he called after them, "try to pin him down…"

"For heaven's sake, Sergeant, he's only a child! Can't be expected to keep some timetable, after all. I mean, it was just playtime for him, that's all. After-dinner playtime. Anyway, he's in bed now. And he needs his rest. And to be perfectly frank, I'm not going to have him exposed to all this. Police all over the beach, and those people standing around gawking. Isn't *our* fault, after all. I mean, the way they lived…"

"Mothers," Krug kept muttering as they trudged back. "Mothers—mothers—*mothers!*"

"All right, Al, I'll talk to her later," Timms said patiently. "Maybe after it quiets down here she'll loosen up a bit."

"How about Rees, sir?" Casey inquired.

"I called that motel, but he isn't there. Nobody's seen him since about seven."

"Yeah," Krug grunted, "and I'll lay you even money—"

"Hey, Lieutenant," the night-tour man named Smithers hollered from the front door. "Got a car full of suitcases in the garage out here. Looks to me like they were about to take off."

They all took a look at the luggage, and a bonus item unseen by Smithers until stronger lights illuminated the back of the Renault: a black straw hat trimmed with sequins which lay wadded into a shapeless bundle on the floor of the car.

"Gets more and more interesting, doesn't it?" Timms commented dryly. "Somebody really wanted us to find the goods, maybe?"

Instead of waiting for the technicians to fingerprint, Timms decided that a search of the house should begin immediately. Krug covered the bedrooms, Casey the rest, including the kitchen which he by-passed until he had finished with the other rooms.

The soapstone drainboard was covered with dirty glasses. Bags of trash sat under the cast-iron sink—emptyings from ashtrays mostly, and many, many dead bottles, both whiskey and wine. Fishing one of the hand-rolled butts out of the trash, Casey sniffed it, confirming that it was cannabis. He slipped the butt into a plastic evidence bag, labeled it and shoved it into his pocket. Then leaning wearily against the sink, he stared around the room, marveling at its self-conscious quaintness. Taken with the rest of the kookily decorated house, it seemed to advertise the sort of life style which, except for a little pot-smoking, would have no connection with crime. An artist's life. Or an artistic craftsman's. Middle-aged swingers tempted by one big ripoff that would set them up for life?

Pushing out through the swinging door, Casey caught a fleeting glimpse of a calendar hanging on the wall. The door had swung closed behind him before his tired perceptions registered that the calendar was last year's.

The hinges squawked as he reversed the door to take another look. Whoever had kept track of the dates here had stopped at May of last year. The picture above the tear-off pages for each month Casey recognized as a bad reproduction of the Gutenberg Bible. *Pater noster qui es.* Pseudo-Gothic printing below the real thing read *Gutenberg to Tantra.*

Printing, Casey's mind skipped. Printer. Printing press... Tantra Press?

The fatigue of fifteen hours on duty forgotten, he plunged through the swinging door again.

TWENTY-FIVE

He drove rapidly, automatically, all mechanical decisions made in some portion of his brain in which judgment and its consequences did not exist. To be moving was enough—a comet trailing horrors. In the congealed darkness of his panic lived only a single idea: to run and run until the nightmare was over.

The Coast Highway south had curved through a short tunnel, becoming the Santa Monica Freeway, a river of traffic enclosed by slanting banks covered with a viny growth. Green-and-white signs had flashed by overhead, informing of exits just beyond to the San Diego Freeway north to Bakersfield and south to Long Beach. Without consideration, Rees had moved into the Long Beach lane, screeching into the exit at high speed, zooming into the stream of southbound traffic which, if he continued, would carry him to the Mexican border.

He passed LA International, a sea of light, a magnet drawing down circling jetliners one by one like dying stars. Beyond lay aerospace complexes, and mile after mile of tract houses, and auto graveyards, and billboards, and neon signs carrying fiery messages of hope, promise, creature comfort if only you ate this, drank that, bought here, saved there—all one and the same to admen, it seemed, for there was something to be sold to everyone, ant and grasshopper alike.

Outlined by thousands of burning electric bulbs, the gigantic refineries of Long Beach looked like light sculptures. Toward the sea, a tall bridge humped black against the harbor glow, an ante-diluvian skeleton. Then the land began to flatten. Dimly aware of a slight shimmying in his front wheels, Rees let up on the gas, but the tremor in the steering wheel continued, and he speeded up again. The only necessity now was to keep moving.

From three blocks away on Main in Ocean Park, they spotted the rooftop flashers of the squad cars which had answered the squeal—two in front, Casey saw as they drew closer, two in the back alley, a fifth angled to block traffic before the inevitable stream of joy-riding rubbernecks arrived to join the street people to whom the district now belonged.

A run-down section of one- and two-story frames and stuccos, the area had been dead until a few years ago, full of faltering little shops, off-beat churches in storefronts, mission houses devoted to saving the souls of a large population of homeless winos. Then the new people had moved in, taking advantage of cheap rents and the built-in custom of their own kind. Every other building was freshly painted now in freaky colors, signs advertising handcrafts, health foods, occult books, psychedelia—all the hip, heavy, *in* endeavors of the dying-planet generation. Peace symbols of every size decorated windows and doors. Through plate glass, collections of exotica from both Near and Far East could be seen. Tantra Press was one of a block of three single-story stucco storefronts painted mud-brown with lavender trim. Next door was a real estate office, and next to that, a cabinetmaker.

Krug was out of the Mustang before Casey set the brake. He nailed the first patrolman he could lay hands on. "Anybody inside there?"

"Not a sign, Sergeant. Looks like you'll need a warrant to get in."

"We got one coming."

Another patrolman ran around the side of the building. "Back door looks like the easiest way in, sir," he reported to Krug.

"Okay, bust it open. But watch yourself," Krug yelled after him as the cop sprinted away again, nearly running down a man wearing a yellow jump suit who had followed him around the building. "Nobody goes in there till I give the word!"

"What's going on here?" demanded the man in the jump suit. "This is my building—"

"Who're you?"

Blinking at Krug's peremptory tone, he meekly confessed that he was the real estate broker. "Harold Hopper. Maybe you've seen my signs. Same location here for twenty-five years, Officer. Never any trouble—"

"You got some now. Want to open that door for us?"

"Be glad to cooperate, of course. But shouldn't I be told—?" He was still talking as Krug took his arm and hustled him over to the lavender-painted door, which had already begun to peel around the Tantra Press sign. "Godwin's not going to like this, me letting you people in without knowing why."

"Keep your teddy-bear suit on, mister, you'll find out soon enough."

The street people standing as silent as store dummies in their funky finery began chanting something as Krug and Casey entered the printshop, followed by two teams of patrolmen. Their voices grew louder and louder, hooting derisively—not mantras, as Casey had first guessed, but a single word, "Bust—bust—*bust!*" over and over again.

But there was no one inside to be busted. The office in front and the printshop in back had been ransacked with a careless, desperate haste.

"Panic time," Krug muttered. "Okay, leave this mess for Harry. Let's nail that real estate hustler before he starts thinking up stories."

But he was due home immediately, Hopper kept protesting when they took him next door to his own office. He ought to call his wife. He'd only dropped by his office to pick up some escrow instructions which had to be delivered early tomorrow morning.

"You can call the missus later," Krug told him. "Right now we want to hear everything you saw or heard going on there today."

"But—Oh, hell, all right." The real estate man turned on lights and started wandering around, seeming fascinated by the photographs of properties hanging on his walls—like hunters' trophies, Casey thought, *This Fine Specimen Bagged.* "Far as I know," Hopper was saying, "he got here the usual time this morning. Godwin, I mean. I didn't see him, y'understand. But I heard that old Renault of his pull up in back."

"Anybody with him?" Krug asked.

"His wife, I guess. Anyway, whoever it was dropped him off and drove away again." He smiled slightly. "Missus probably had a hangover. Or maybe they had a fight. Been a lot of that the past few months. Something about another woman, I think."

"How about locks changed?" Casey said. "Anything like that the past few months?"

Hopper nodded. "Last December, I think it was. Had a hell of a time getting duplicate keys out of him, too. Said he was working on some special job. Something valuable, I guess. Anyway, he practically made me swear on a stack of Bibles I wouldn't let anybody—" He stopped abruptly. "Hey, for God's sake, it isn't *dirty* stuff, is it? Pornographic stuff he's been printing?"

Krug eyed him coldly. "You saying you never got a look at what he was working on?"

"How could I with everything locked up in those—" Again he stopped. "Listen, I don't bother my tenants unless they're late on their rent."

"How about employees or partners?" Casey asked. "Can you give us any names, Mr. Hopper?"

"Well, he used to have this kid come in sometimes for rush orders. But he canned him, I guess. Got a new fella in regular since the first of the year." He scratched a bald spot, disarranging the strands of hair which carefully covered it. "Come to think of it, though, I haven't seen him around since Sunday."

"Godwin's open Sundays?"

"Not usually. That's why I got to wondering when this Jerry showed up. Jerry Something, can't remember if I ever heard his last name. Young fella with a beard. One of those motorcycle maniacs. Didn't strike me as the kind of help you could trust."

Jervis Godwin had been his tenant for ten years, he told them. A reliable, hard-working sort of a guy with what looked like a nice little business. Mostly local printing, handbills and stationery for the neighborhood merchants. Nothing anybody could get rich on, but a good enough living. His wife kept the books and he ran the press. A real Mom and Pop deal. The last people in the world you'd expect anything—

"But come to think of it," he interrupted himself, "something hit him a couple, three years ago. The youth bug, I guess you'd call it. Anyhow, Godwin started hanging around the kid places, and it rubbed off, I guess. Grew himself a beard. Stopped having his hair cut. Pretty soon I see him showing up for work in jeans and sandals like some hippie or something."

"What happened Sunday?" Krug prodded him. "With this Jerry you were talking about."

"Well, I'm open weekends. Got to be when you're in the real estate game. It's like I tell my wife, you're a preacher or a broker, Sunday's for sure no day of rest!" He seemed to expect laughter, and not getting it, went on less willingly: "Like I say, Godwin's closed Sunday. So when I saw this Jerry out back fooling with the door—"

"Trying to get in, you mean?"

"That's what it looked like to me. Anyhow, I figured I better phone Godwin, just to make sure."

"What kind of a reaction did you get?"

"Thanks for nothing." Hopper grinned. "But I noticed he showed up plenty fast, so for sure something fishy was going on..."

Fifteen minutes later when they returned next door, they found Harry Berger busily rooting through a pile of trash heaped in one corner of the printshop. "This dreck case," he snarled over his shoulder. "I miss the last inning of the Dodgers' replay—and for what?" He tossed scraps of paper in the air. "This garbage."

Catching one of the paper cuttings floating around like confetti, Casey fingered its crackling texture. "Looks like evidence to me, Harry. Isn't this—?"

"Treasury paper, or the nearest thing to it. Yes, indeedy, Mr. Sherlock, sir." Berger pushed himself up from his squatting position. "All the equipment's here. But where the fuck has all the *goods* gone, will you tell me that?" He gestured toward the line of steel lock-type cabinets lining one wall. "Every one of those is a Mother Hubbard's cupboard!"

"According to the landlord next door, Godwin started loading what he said was a big rush order this morning," Krug told him. "Later on—he couldn't say what time exactly—another guy showed up to help him. Big guy, he claims. A bruiser. Couldn't give us a description, just some muscles, that's all."

"Between the two of them," Casey added, "they evidently packed the whole score in cardboard cartons and loaded them in a U-Haul truck."

"So we check all the U-Haul rental joints for fifty miles around?" Berger sighed. "Well, it's some kind of a cockamamie lead, I guess."

In a coffee can lid which had been used as an ashtray, they found six filter-tip butts and the chewed stub of the same sort of small cigar which Krug smoked. "Be interesting to see if the saliva tests match," Casey commented as he slipped it into an evidence envelope. "One here, three at the Roche apartment—"

"Don't rush it, partner. We got all we can handle right now without the dreamboat stuff."

Timms arrived shortly after this, his square somber face gray with fatigue. He had persuaded the Godwins' neighbor, Mrs. Killigrew, to make an identification of the body, he told them while he walked around inspecting the printshop. As they had surmised, the decedent was indeed Jervis Godwin. The hospital would not permit any visitors in the surgical intensive care ward, but Mrs. Killigrew's description of Godwin's wife—her name was Emrie—gave them an almost certain make on the wounded woman. "Still alive, but only barely," he reported gloomily. "While they were wheeling her into the operating room, she came to for a couple seconds. Nurse I talked to said she was trying to say something. Sounded like gobbledegook to her. All she could make out was something about somebody or something being ready."

Krug grimaced. "That's a big help."

"Doctors say if she survives we'll be damn lucky to get a statement of any kind before next week sometime. So that's that." Timms turned his attention to Berger. "Looks like your pigeons flew, Harry."

"Like eagles, Lieutenant. All we've got here is some tail feathers." He had already reported to the feds downtown, Berger added—meaning downtown Los Angeles. Agents would be rousing U-Haul rental proprietors all over the west district for the rest of the night. The two Treasury men they had met with before were on their way here right now. The night promised to be a long one.

Briefly, Krug covered what they had found out from the real estate man then. Next move, he said, they would take Hopper to the station for a look at mug shots. A dim hope—but all they had so far—that Godwin's musclebound helper might be on file.

"Better split up," Timms advised. "You take Hopper, Al. Kellog can cover that cabinetmaker and anybody else around here who might know something." He glanced at his watch. "Let's lock it up in a couple hours and meet at the station."

Picturing Krug seated comfortably at his own desk with a cup of coffee in front of him and perhaps even a stale sandwich out of the vending machine downstairs, Casey zigzagged the Mustang through Ocean Park, cursing the long-deceased developers who had laid out these crazy-quilt subdivisions, chopping off streets here, avenues there, making a mouse-in-a-maze of anyone trying to drive through. And of course there weren't any public phones around. Naturally, he thought bitterly. Even if he did find one he'd probably discover that he didn't have a dime.

But he did, as it happened. Not one but two ten-cent pieces in his pocket. And at the corner of Lincoln and a narrow side street without a name sign, he spied a neighborhood liquor store with a booth outside.

Her phone rang and rang depressingly. The most bleak and lonely sound he'd ever heard. Then she mumbled "Hello" sleepily.

"Joey, I'm sorry—I tried to reach you hours ago—"

"Did you?" flatly.

"About six, I think it was."

"That's a long time between phone booths."

"I know, but I couldn't—"

"All right, so what happened? That is if one may ask."

"Look, I don't blame you for being angry—"

"Didn't say I was. Merely asked what happened. And please," she added, "don't patronize me."

"I'm sorry, I didn't mean to." Casey drew a deep breath, aware that he was perspiring now, profusely. "All I meant— Well, anyway, I'm glad you're not mad at me. You see, this case we've been working on started to break a while ago. Couldn't call you after the first time. Not till now, I mean. It's this weirdo counterfeit—Well, never mind," he sighed. "Policeman's lot, et cetera. All I can say is I'm sorry about this evening."

"All right."

Casey listened to her soft breathing. All right—meaning what? he wondered. That's that, enough of cops? "Joey, I'd really like to try again. Like sometime soon when I'm sure I can—"

"Do that," she said distantly, and hung up.

Well, at least I finally got hold of her, Casey thought. But leaning against the glass side of the phone booth, listening to the dial tone, he found small comfort in the idea. Try again. *Do that,* she'd said. And he hadn't the remotest hint whether she meant encouragement or a put-down. Wouldn't know, he realized, until he did try again. Not exactly, he thought sadly, what you'd call a replay of *Love Story.*

The cabinetmaker, who was also Hopper's tenant, lived in the end unit of a one-story stucco apartment building staggered like children's blocks up a steep rise. Lights were still burning, and in the open garage which separated the cabinetmaker's apartment from his next-door neighbor's stood a battered-looking Ford panel delivery truck. Neat but unprofessional lettering on the rear loading door advertised *S. T. "Swede" Olsen—Cabinetmaker— Your Yob Is My Yob.*

No dour Svenska this, Casey decided as he punched the doorbell. Can't help but make my yob a little easier. But the idea did little for his state of mind. "Yah—" He heard an angry voice yelling inside. "Who's dere?" And Casey's spirits hit bottom. The whole world was obviously in conspiracy to down him.

"Have to excuse me," Olsen kept saying when Casey finally managed to gain entrance into the apartment. "But I didn't hear no sireen. And you got no uniform on. How'm I gonna know you're a real policeman, hah?"

"Mr. Olsen, I showed you my badge and ID card—"

"But, dammit, young fella, you don't look like no cop!"

Try me twenty years from now. Picturing a beefy, balding fortyish self, Casey sighed glumly. But his voice was mild, consciously patient as he said, "Let's get back to today, Mr. Olsen. You got to your shop about eight to pick up some cabinets. You delivered and installed them, and got back about—what time?"

"Maybe noon." The homely horse-faced cabinetmaker shrugged indifferently. "Like always, I stop for dinner on the way."

"Was the U-Haul truck parked in the alley behind Tantra Press when you got back to your shop?"

"Nah, that was later on I seen it. When I went out for a beer." He grinned slightly, showing yellowish teeth, an exact color match with his thick, lank home-barbered hair. "Used to be it was whiskey, but I only drink the beer now. Baby stuff," he added contemptuously. "Drink a quart, piss a gallon. Guess you think that's all an old coot like me is good for, huh?" He waited expectantly, but experienced with this sort of fishing common to the aging sexual braggart, Casey kept silent. But Olsen persisted: "You want to guess how old I am? Come on, take a guess. Let me tell you, young fella, you be surprised, I bet you! All the girls, I tell 'em, they're surprised."

"For Chrissake, I figured you eloped with the guy," Krug snarled when Casey dragged into the squad room almost two hours later. "What'd you run into at Olsen's, an orgy or something?"

"Uh-hunh." Casey flopped into his desk chair. "Trouble was, it was all in his head." He fished out his notebook, flipping pages. "What would you prefer to hear first, Al? I've got it all here. 'Four times with Myrtle on Friday night.' Incidentally, I have her phone number and vital statistics. 'Three times with'—"

"Okay, okay, I get the picture—an old fart with a big imagination. What else did you get?"

"He buddied a little with Barrett at the local pub. Stud stuff mostly, I imagine. But Barrett dropped some hints once in a while. Big-shot line. He'd be in the bread soon, et cetera. Olsen figured him for as big a put-on as he is, I guess. Oh, and I checked out the beer joint too," he added before Krug could ask. "Seems somebody was making discreet inquiries about Tantra Press yesterday. Could be the feds, maybe."

"Yeah, Hopper talked to 'em, too. Said he figured they were Internal Revenue snoops." He chewed on a pencil, staring into space. "One of the plainclothes boys from Narco picked up word from some beardo-freaks who were mousing around that alley this afternoon. They claim a woman delivered the U-Haul. Blonde, they said. Funky-looking, whatever that means. Probably Godwin's wife." He tossed the pencil aside. "You got any word about our muscleman?"

"Nothing that helps much. Guy had dark hair, Olsen claims. Jump suits must be big around there, he was wearing a brown one. But maybe Olsen meant coveralls. Anyway, he was a real Goliath type. Handled cartons that Godwin could hardly lift as if they were marshmallows." He scrutinized Krug, who was leaning back in his swivel chair now, hands clasped behind his head. No good news there. "Hopper couldn't make him?"

"Nope, not even a nibble." He kept chewing the inside of his cheek—a sure sign of suppressed emotion. "Got word back on Rees a while ago. 'Exemplary behavior.' Nice, hah? Kept to himself mostly. Cellmate was an embezzler with no previous criminal record." He kept staring at the ceiling, the muscles along his jaws moving rhythmically, like pulse points. "That son of a bitch," he said softly. "He may think he's clean, but I'm gonna nail him yet. Sure as God made little green apples, I'm gonna nail that mother for a long walk."

TWENTY-SIX

His mind seemed to be operating at a great distance now, moving clumsily, imprecisely, around his immediate problems. He must stop for gas soon. And he was in need of a comfort station. Some place with food, Rees decided vaguely, although he was not hungry.

An old stake truck passed him, the back jammed with long-haired college-age kids, all waving their arms and singing something. Jesus freaks? Their voices were snatched away in the high-speed roar before he could identify their song. Something from *Jesus Christ, Superstar* probably. *Hosannah! Heysannah!* The new disciples, he thought, free, young, confident. Had he ever felt that way? He could not remember. The decade between his own age and theirs seemed a long voyage into another country.

Sickening waves of deep physical alarm kept rising in him, unreadable messages from the limbo beyond panic. What am I doing? he wondered suddenly. Running. But from what to what? If I cross any border, I'll be a fugitive.

Like a membrane tearing, his mind opened then, flooded with an intense anxious awareness of himself and his actions. He saw an exit marked *Roadside Business*, and swung off, feeling the Volkswagen drifting dangerously on the curve before he could slow and shift down. Recognizing the interior ghost as an old one—fatalism as dense and unthinking as instinct—he braked hard. Fatalism with a new face now, he thought as his tires squealed and the chassis rocked. Self-destructiveness. The other thing Stevens had warned him against.

"It may look like something else, Paul," the parole officer had said. "Anything from righteous anger to a desire to play hookey. It takes lots of forms. But what it really is, is hopelessness. You set yourself up in situations which inevitably lead to one fall after another."

Like that side trip to Tahoe, he thought bleakly as he pulled into the floodlit parking area for a motel-coffeeshop-gas-station complex. Like fastening himself blindly to Susannah. Like setting up Krug as some cruel force before which he would always be prostrate, helpless.

He climbed out of the Volkswagen stiffly, slamming the door. The two blood-drenched bodies burned like coals in his mind, and leaning against the car, knees and hands shaking badly, he lit a cigarette. Murder. Hopelessness. The words seemed truths in another language—murder too incredible, hopelessness too dire—only half understood. But the full meaning of "fugitive" grasped him like claws, ripping the thick spurious skin of fatalism. The loser's disease, he thought. He had not realized how profoundly prison had altered his thinking.

Trying to remember how he had thought and acted when he was an ordinary citizen—not lonely and frightened, plagued by a sense that he had lost contact with the world—he found that memory failed him. Had he always, in some way, been running, then? Could be, Rees decided. Because running men are friendless, aren't they? And he had discovered, when Ellen died, that there was no one to call for help. No family, no long-time friends anywhere—the result of a life style traveling here and there for years, working for foreign companies. In his intense happiness with Ellen, he had never asked himself why change had always seemed more desirable to him than advancement. Gypsies, his wife had called them. International gypsies, the new breed.

Or an old breed of rootless beings? he wondered. Was it alien-ation, a secret dread of responsibility, settling down, which had kept him moving two years here, three there? All those sleepless nights in prison, he had turned the questions over and over in his mind, but he had never arrived at any answers. Only that he had been happy. Only that. Even when it is gone forever, he had discovered, joy stubbornly resists analysis.

Tossing the cigarette away, Rees looked at his watch. It was almost ten and a long way back. He opened the car door again. First, he told himself savagely, get rid of the goddam plastic bag. And tomorrow tell the whole crazy story to your new PO More than anyone, a parole officer must understand the parolee's problem of police persecution.

Fishing blindly, his fingertips found the small, smooth plastic bundle lying on the floor between the back and front seats. But it was heavier than he expected, something solid and weighty inside now with the pieces of cardboard. His heart expanding, then contracting painfully, Rees tipped up the bag, and with a soft thump a handgun slid out. A gleaming nickel-silvered pistol.

TWENTY-SEVEN

"Okay, Barrett shows up at the printshop Sunday," Lieutenant Timms began to lay it out again, piece by piece. "The printer, Godwin, gets a call from his landlord, and hightails it over there. But Godwin doesn't know yet that Barrett's already blown their caper, so he probably plays it cool. This is a partner, after all. And they're almost ready to make their big move. Stands to reason Godwin probably sicked the girl onto Barrett to find out what he was up to. And then the fat was in the fire."

"They had a thing going, the snapshot proves that," Krug agreed. "And Barrett was a fool for anything in skirts. So if he spilled to her he'd blown it—Well, you can see what'd happen. He'd been filching enough paper he had the price of a getaway. All she had to do was talk up a rendezvous somewhere later to keep him around till they could deal with him."

"A real nebbish crook, this guy." Harry Berger grinned at Casey. "What every young cop should learn, right? Crime only pays the smart guys. But okay," he went on, yawning, "so much for putting it together. The feds are covering all the U-Haul rental places. So we wait till they find something to follow up, right? What they figure so far is five people in on it. All amateurs, probably. A nice little deal somebody put together." And he began to enumerate: "Barrett with the plates and photo-reproduction stuff. Godwins with the press. The girl with something—maybe the brains, for all we know. For sure she had the guts! The fifth one probably has the syndicate contacts. Maybe furnished the financing all these months."

"Wouldn't make any bets then on his amateur status," Krug grunted. "Could be four little Indians and one chief."

"Plus a mysterious visitor to the Godwins'," Casey added. "Unless the kid who saw him is lying, he can't be our killer—so who is he? The ME says they were shot at least three hours before the visitor showed up."

No clear prints had been identified yet at the Godwin house, Timms told them. Two night-tour men were trying to locate Paul Rees to see if he could identify the raincoat they had found at the Godwin house as the one the girl had been wearing at the scene of the Barrett homicide. No sign of the murder gun as yet, so an assumption that the killer had carried it away with him was valid so far. An APB on the U-Haul truck had gone out immediately, but Timms felt that Godwin's helper could be the coolest one of the five. He had probably stashed the counterfeit money and would lie low till the heat was off. Or, if he had run it right away, he had probably transferred the load to another vehicle.

"Probably a local drop," Harry Berger declared. "Makes more sense than chancing a stop with a load like that." Taking a liberty which any of the detectives in the squad wouldn't have dared with a stickler like Timms, he perched on the corner of the lieutenant's desk, staring across the half-deserted squad room. "Say it took them a couple hours or so to pack it," he went on thoughtfully. "Another hour or so to load the truck." Taking a note pad out of his pocket, he began figuring. "Must be somewhere in the neighborhood of fifteen to twenty cartons to take that length of time. Maybe fifty pounds apiece?" As he talked, he did sums rapidly, looking more and more discouraged. "Could be a record-breaker we've got here. If I'm anywhere close, fifteen to twenty good-sized cartons could hold something like eight to ten million dollars in blocks of twenties."

"Jesus," Krug breathed. "No wonder those Treasury guys're running around in circles."

Peddled at a discount, Berger went on, the haul figured to split into something like a quarter of a million dollars each for the five counterfeiters—after discounting, that is. "So our killer's ending up with over a million, right? Nice work," he muttered. "If you got the stomach for it."

"What bothers me," Timms said, "is where that U-Haul got to. With an APB out, we'd have a pickup by now if he was still on the road."

They agreed that the truck was probably hidden somewhere, possibly the load already transferred to another vehicle. Their only hope of a lead lay in locating the U-Haul truck.

"Some hope," Krug commented sourly. "Godwin's wife probably rented the damn thing. Nothing to tie it from there, right? So all he has to do is leave it on the street somewhere. Unless we nail him in that truck, it's a dead end."

TWENTY-EIGHT

From a public phone booth outside the coffeeshop where he had stopped, Rees dialed the Pelican Motel direct, sweating as he listened to the ringing at the other end. Let it be the woman. Getting around the gossipy manager would only waste—

"Good evening, Pelican Motel."

Thank God. "This is Paul Rees. I have Room—"

"Number Eleven, yes," she acknowledged pleasantly. "What can I do for you, Mr. Rees?"

"Well, it may sound silly—" No, wrong tack. He cleared his throat and started again. "When I was in there earlier this evening—you remember?—you mentioned something about my car."

"Sounds like you're having more trouble with it. Golly, isn't it awful trying to get anything fixed these days?"

"Then you saw someone?" Don't flog it, she's already given you the cue. "Like a mechanic, I mean," he added hastily. "Someone working on my car?"

"Well, I don't know about working." She sounded amused. "But he was a mechanic, all right. You know those dirty old coveralls they always wear. And he had a toolbox with him." He heard her sighing. "Probably closed now, Mr. Rees. But if you remember the name of the place—"

A mythical garage. Yes, he would try calling them, he told her. No problem, he was an Auto Club member. As he thanked her and hung up, an uncontrollable shivering seized him, the sort of mindless terror of the unknown which he had not experienced since he was a child. While he'd been sleeping this afternoon, someone had planted the gun. Not the police, he knew now, but someone even more dangerous to him. Whoever it was who had searched his room yesterday. A murderer.

He was afraid to touch the gun, afraid to leave it in the car, but even more afraid of carrying it. Poking it back into the plastic bag with his knuckles, Rees shoved the bundle under the front seat on the driver's side. Then he risked a fast trip into the coffee shop, which was almost empty, smelling of charcoal-broiled hamburgers and some sort of pine-scented floor cleaner. "Just coffee, please," he said to the waitress, and headed for the restroom.

His face in the men's room mirror was tallow-colored, he noticed vaguely—frighteningly, nakedly desperate. Eyes dilated. Veins pulsing in his temples. Urine boiled out of him hot as acid, and he couldn't stop shaking. For God's sake, he told himself—as he washed his hands, splashed his face with cold water—get hold of yourself. Yes, it's a nightmare. But this time it isn't yours. So this time there has to be a way out of it.

His coffee was sitting on the counter when he came out—steaming hot and stale-smelling, too hot to drink. Didn't matter, Rees thought, he couldn't swallow anyway. Something sticking in his craw, as Ellen, a country girl, used to say. A planted gun. Possibly a murder weapon. And no one to help, least of all the police.

"Anything wrong with your coffee?"

"What? Oh, no, it's fine, thanks."

The waitress drifted off, wiping the counter slowly, humming under her breath with the canned music issuing through ceiling speakers.

The tune was familiar—Nashville sound—and after a moment, Rees realized where he had heard it lately. At the Godwins' party. Over and over again, the same song. *Ooo-wow-you-scare-me.* His heart clenched. *Play it for giggles, Jervy.*

As the music twanged, his mind kept turning the fragments like a kaleidoscope: Godwin and the coat Susannah had worn… Witness in the alley…Hit-and-run…Her boyfriend…Godwin trying to tell her something…*Keep living dangerously…What you can't see…*

The wheeling, whirling in his brain ceased suddenly, and spellbound, he saw the clear space. Space which, with luck, he might operate in with some degree of safety. Find out something. Even a thread would help.

Not your nightmare, he told himself again as he left a half dollar on the counter. So there's got to be a way out. Five minutes later he was on the freeway again, headed north.

TWENTY-NINE

"So all we've got going for us now is Rees." Lieutenant Timms's eyes kept swiveling from Krug to Casey, appearing like eggs over-poached in some purple-brown substance. "If he can identify that raincoat, he can probably make the hat, too. And he told you she picked it up at the party—those were his exact words, right?"

Repetition, Casey thought. The art of detecting was a matter of endless repetitive conversations. The clock on the squad-room wall said eleven-thirty. He yawned to cover his unconscious groan. Another hour to go yet, at least, before he could possibly finish typing the day's reports. They never told you at the Academy how much time you'd spend parked in front of typewriters. How many hours you'd waste waiting for developments. Or how many girls you'd lose because of the damned waiting—

"Here's your news," one of the night-tour men announced as he walked into the squad room. "Just picked up this little goodie from our local witch doctor." He pitched a large brown envelope onto Krug's desk.

But it was Timms who scanned the report inside first. "Final PM on Roche," he muttered, scowling. "Listen to this."

As he began to read aloud, all the tiny hairs on Casey's skin stirred uneasily—an atavistic reaction to the horror implied in the cold, technical post-mortem language. What it boiled down to, as Timms was saying, was a severe manhandling of the decedent before death. Deep contusions on both upper arms—hand marks from the shape. It looked, he said, like some strong-arm had grabbed her from behind with a paralyzing grip. Which meant either a maniac or some muscle type as strong as a gorilla. There was a good possibility that Susannah Roche had been thrown bodily out the window.

Another murder as crazy as killing a man with his own car."

"You get the picture," the lieutenant was saying unemotionally. "What we're up against is a real ironball killer."

"A nut case, you mean," Krug grunted.

"Or a guy so scared and greedy, it amounts to the same thing."

"Could be that the timing figures somehow," Casey mused aloud, unaware at first that he was interrupting. "Something queer about that gap between the time the U-Haul left Tantra and the Godwins were—" But no one was listening.

"How it went, maybe," Timms's steady magisterial voice overrode his, "one thing led to another. They wasted Barrett because he blew their deal. But they had a witness to that—Rees. Then a fast phone call gave them the news we had the murder car, too." He leaned against Krug's desk, rubbing his end-of-the-day whiskers. "Driver probably figured we could connect Roche with Barrett sooner or later, so he didn't waste any time getting to her. On the other hand, he took the time to make it look like suicide—which makes me think he still wasn't scared. But by the time he got to the Godwins—Well, never mind that," he interrupted himself. "Next move is Rees. He's all we've got going for us," he repeated, "so the sooner we get him in here the better."

But ten minutes later even that hope was blasted.

"Just took a call for you fellas," the manager informed Casey and Krug when they walked into the Pelican Motel office. "Police, right? Said you should phone as soon as you got here." They usually charged a quarter for phone service, he explained while he dialed from the small switchboard behind the counter which held a cash register, stacks of brochures printed by the Santa Monica Chamber of Commerce, a plaque from some motel association and an ivory-colored house phone. But seeing this was official—"Police Department? Hold on a second."

Krug lifted the ivory-colored receiver, handing it to Casey. "Be my guest."

"Thanks, partner. Yeah, Kellog," Casey said into the receiver. "What's up?"

"Logged in an anonymous call a couple minutes ago the lieutenant said you guys'd be interested in." Casey recognized the gravel voice of the duty sergeant. "Party that lives near that Coast Highway house, so he or she claimed. Voice could be a woman. Anyhow, he was out for the evening, he claims. Just got home and heard about the shooting from the neighbors."

"Any reason for the anonymity?"

"The usual crap about not wanting to be involved. But he claims he saw what might be your killer."

Hell, Casey thought despondently as he listened to the description, there goes my certified Sherlock button. "Seems we're at the right place at the wrong time, Al." He banged the receiver. "See you outside for a minute?" He hustled his partner out the door. "A tall dark-haired man about thirty was seen driving away from the Godwin house in a blue Volkswagen."

"Rees, sure as hell!"

"But the time's wrong, Al. At the time the witness is talking about, we were here with Rees."

"So give or take a half hour, how long you think it takes to pull a trigger? Anyway, you ever know a witness to get anything right?" Krug looked feverish now, boiling with excitement. "Christ, the nerve of the guy! He's got the balls of a—But he really blew it, didn't he? When he gave us that 'E and J Godwin' bit? Blew his own cover-up. And you remember how he was sweating when he opened the door?"

Promise of a warrant on the way did little at first to convince the motel manager. "But how can he be gone when he's paid up for the night?" he kept insisting. "People don't—Well, listen, he didn't say anything—"

"Joe, tell them about his phone call," an unseen woman called through the half-open inner door which connected the motel office with living quarters. "If he's in trouble of some kind—"

"Yeah, that's right, I forgot. Rees called here a while ago. Something about his car, the wife said. Squawking about some mechanic—which don't surprise me any. Guy was only here five minutes, she said. Probably charged Rees a fortune."

"So that's his worry, right?" Krug jerked a thumb toward the Plexiglas outer door. "Come on, don't give us a hard time."

With the draperies drawn, lamps burning, Rees's motel room had a kind of transient coziness as shallow and false as the pictures on the walls. Crumpled newspapers lay scattered on the floor. The bedspread was wrinkled where someone had sat on it. An ashtray on the nightstand overflowed with cigarette butts. In the bathroom a faucet drip-dripped monotonously.

Krug tried the closet first. "Clothes're still here." He started going through the pockets while Casey peered into the bathroom.

"All his shaving gear's here, Al. Toothbrush and so forth."

"Don't mean a thing, he's got the dough to buy more." Krug's voice was muffled, for he was on his hands and knees now, poking under the bed. "Nothing but house moss here." Groaning softly, he straightened and began pulling the bed apart, tossing the covers in a heap—an old police technique of random ransack-search which, to Casey's mind, had always seemed excessive.

But even so, there was something exciting in his partner's furious energy, and Casey quickly went through the bureau drawers, one by one, searching under neatly stacked shirts, socks, underwear. In a bottom drawer was the jumble of miscellaneous items which Rees had dumped out of his bags when they had picked them up for fingerprinting this morning. Among them was a manila envelope which Casey opened, finding escrow papers from a property sale, some letters and pictures which were personal and a passport made out to Ellen Hollis Rees and Paul Joseph Rees, husband and wife. Inspecting the deceased wife's passport-picture smile, Casey tried to imagine the loss, but grief was as yet unknown to him. Probably in the flesh she'd been even prettier, he decided. One of those quiet passionate helpmeets. The old-fashioned word brought a twinge of longing which made him feel callow and silly. He riffled quickly through the passport. "Looks like they used to travel a lot." There was no reply from Krug. "Here are his parole papers. He's due to report at nine tomorrow."

"Fat chance. Son of a bitch's probably across the Mexican border by now."

"Without his passport?"

"Hell, you can travel all over mañana-land on a tourist card. Buy a fake one for ten bucks." Like a ragpicker with competition, Krug was tearing through the closet again. "Pair of shoes here. Old ones, looks like, no loss there. Shoe box on the floor." Casey heard him puffing as he squatted for a look. "No store label. Lid's gone. Looks brand-new." He straightened again, grunting. "Nothing in his pockets is the giveaway. Bastard probably cleaned 'em out before he split."

"But it doesn't make sense, Al. Why would he phone?"

"Ah, come on, use your head. He's playing for time."

"But leaving all his stuff—"

"Wouldn't you if you figured it'd give you a lead of maybe twelve, thirteen, fourteen hours? He don't know somebody spotted that Volks, we'd be getting an APB out on him. Probably figures the first we'll tumble is when he don't show up at Parole in the morning."

It sounded logical, Casey had to admit. But logic didn't usually enter into homicides. "Al, it doesn't work," he said ten minutes later as he pulled into the section behind the City Hall marked OFFICIAL VEHICLES ONLY and they crawled out of the

Mustang for what seemed the thousandth time that day. "Either Rees has flipped, or somebody's doing a number on us. Who we should be hunting right now is that anonymous caller."

Krug's raspberry was eloquently loud and insulting. Good old Uncle Al, the Emperor of Put-Down. "You want coffee? I'll buy."

Entering headquarters, they detoured down the corridor to the vending machines. As usual, Krug griped about the cream which wasn't real anymore, settling for black with lots of sugar. The coffee smelled like stewed inner tubes as always, but it was burning hot and welcome. They both sipped cautiously, then headed for the stairs.

"The fact remains," Casey said stubbornly, "we haven't anything but circumstances and that anonymous call to connect Rees."

"Bullshit." Krug slumped into his swivel desk chair.

Opposite him, Casey hunched over his coffee, brooding. "Just take a look at what the guy's been up against, Al. He's a witness to a murder. Then his room gets searched. But when he reports it to us, all we do is hassle him, because by this time we've not only caught up with his record, his chick's dead, too. All of a sudden he's a prime suspect." Krug started to growl, but Casey persisted. "Whoever searched his room must've spotted those parole papers, Al. Saw he had a natural for a setup of some kind. And if he's desperate for time—Well, isn't it possible he could be using Rees as a red herring?"

"For Chrissake, you and your goddam theories." Krug gulped his coffee and crushed the cup. "Red herring." His laughter blared like a brass horn. "Go back and read the book, genius. Like the part where it tells about following evidence."

"Instead of steering it, you mean."

"Who's steering? I'm not"

"Not unless you have to, anyway."

Krug sucked in a breath, expelling it violently. "Now you listen to me, college boy, and you listen good. I been a cop for as long as you been living, you get me? A *cop*. Which means I've seen every kind of two-bit hustler by now. I've smelled every kind of nickel-a-bunch crook. I've listened to every kind of shithead phony that's ever come down the pike. What I'm talking about is experience—get me, genius? Police experience. Something you haven't got much of yet, and don't you ever forget it! We stick with what we got, and what we got now is Rees—right? Now, get busy on the reports," he finished sullenly. "I'll hit up the watch commander for a plainclothes team to stake out the Pelican."

THIRTY

Serves you damn well right, Casey thought as his partner stamped out and down the stairs again. He kept leafing through his notebook, trying to concentrate. But his brain was like a fist closed tight around resentment and rage at his own stupidity. Instead of persuading Al, making him see the possibility could conceivably exist that Rees was being used, he'd started an idiotic mini-war which could go on for days, even weeks.

Time, he kept thinking. Has to figure somehow. That gap between clearing out Tantra Press and killing the Godwins *must* mean something. Delay of some kind? Or a change of plan? If something had pinned down the killer, for instance...But this was the wildest kind of guessing, he knew.

His coffee had gone cold by this time. Depressed by the idea of all the typing he faced, Casey pocketed his notebook and trudged down the stairs for a fresh cup from the vending machine. But he pushed the wrong button, *cream* instead of *black,* and seething as he watched the pale liquid flowing into the paper cup behind the glassed-in slot, he decided to punish himself by drinking it. He was halfway through the bland unsatisfying cup, beginning to focus again, when the sense of a pattern began to emerge in his mind. He hadn't quite pinned it down when Harry Berger called.

"Good news, *bubi*. Our fearless feds may have a line on that U-Haul truck."

"That's fast work."

"Why not? They got a hundred guys out ringing doorbells." His voice quickened. "Hey, remember that Narco spook's newsy little bit about some blond dame delivering the truck? Well, it looks like it might be kosher. Because a blonde rented one late this morning from a place on Lincoln. Guy said she wanted a van, but he didn't have any, so she settled for the truck. Anyway, she gave a fake address. Claimed she'd forgotten her driver's license, but she sweet-talked the guy into letting her have it anyway. After she paid in advance, that is, plus a huge deposit."

"What's the description?"

"I told you, *bubi*, blonde—what else d'you want?"

"A description, Harry."

"Okay, Sherlock. Maybe thirty years old. Plenty of face paint, the guy said, so he couldn't really tell. But around thirty. Sort of skinny, he said, but plenty of pizzazz. Ankle-strap platforms and a groovy dress. Hair was out of a bottle, he figured. About shoulder length—"

Scribbling frantically in his notebook, Casey got it all down. And after he hung up, he studied what he had written, a slow excitement beginning to stir in him. No mistaking that somebody, somewhere along the line, was seeing wrong.

Ten minutes later, at Santa Monica Hospital, he was explaining that he realized he couldn't talk to the patient: "Mrs. Emrie Godwin? What I need is her vital statistics. A police matter."

While he waited for the woman who was obviously the senior nurse to inspect his badge and ID card, he glanced cautiously around the ward, intimidated by the deadly quiet, the cool incurious scrutiny of the nursing team. Surgical Intensive Care was dimly lit, heavily carpeted, curtained into cubicles positioned like spokes in a half-circle wheel around the electronic console where the nurses sat like astronauts, monitoring pulsing signals from each fragile, ailing human mechanism adrift in the dark limbo of life or death. The opposite of my job,

Casey was thinking when he became aware of the nurse's soft murmur.

"—All here on her Emergency Admittance." She handed him the aluminum-backed hospital chart. "Help yourself. It's the bottom page."

As quietly as he was able, Casey flipped through the chart. And squinting in the insufficient light, he read the Jane Doe identification: height approx. 5'7", weight approx. 155 lbs., age approx. 50 years, eyes blue, hair blond, complexion fair, scars as follows—

"That was quick," the nurse commented when he handed her the chart. "What'd she do to get herself shot up like that?"

"Don't know yet. This is just routine." Casey smiled his thanks and pushed out through the padded door into the hospital corridor. For sure the one thing Mrs. Godwin had not done was rent a U-Haul truck this morning.

THIRTY-ONE

Staying on the northbound San Diego Freeway instead of branching off onto the westbound connecting artery to Santa Monica, Rees by-passed the small city's eastern limits, continuing on to the Sunset Boulevard exit. The famous scenic boulevard, lined with huge houses on deep garden lots, wound westward, he knew. The longest way around, to be sure. But, he hoped, the safest.

Panic had settled now into a slow, heavy fear-pulse in him. How much time? he kept wondering. How long could he stay free? Once the police had him, any chance of aiding himself would be finished—Krug would see to that. But whoever had planted the gun—

His mind veered crazily. Like a formula, he thought. Not chemistry, physics. Between X, the unknown factor, and Y, the known force, anything caught must experience *ohm*-pressures at a ratio calculated—

He groaned aloud. Just get there, for Chrissake. *Get there.* When you've only one chance to save yourself, it doesn't take any intellectualizing to prove the simple fact that you're desperate.

"—So there's *six,* not five," Casey shouted over the persistent buzzing on the telephone line, his mouth full of bread and paper-thin ham. "Four men and *two* women. And listen, Al, I've got another idea about that, too—"

"Save it, we'll get our answers from Rees when we nail him."

"No, listen to me! They must've planned a rendezvous later somewhere. But something went wrong—"

"Save it, I said. I'm heading home."

Casey choked down the mouthful. "At least give me a chance to tell you, Al. Because it all begins to fit now. So wait'll I get there? Five minutes," he added before Krug could speak, and hung up. But the promised five minutes stretched into fifteen while he made two more calls—both inquiries, which he hoped sounded casual enough to conceal their information-gathering purpose.

He had parked in a red zone on Sixteenth, getting into the hospital through an Employees Only entrance which he'd overshot on his way out, discovering instead this small visitors' foyer, which was a policeman's dream—not only public phones, but also a tempting array of vending machines lined against one wall, each dispensing something different, from sandwiches to fresh fruit. Sophisticated machines which even made change.

Shoving an apple in his pocket, juggling the milk and sandwich he had also purchased, Casey pushed out through the swing door onto the quiet street. Milk sloshed out of the carton, dribbling down his front. The half sandwich he was trying to gobble as he ran crumbled into fragments. So much for dinner, he thought bitterly, licking his fingers. But he gulped the balance of the milk before he climbed into his Mustang, tossing the empty carton in the gutter—according to city littering ordinances, a fifty-dollar fine.

Krug was waiting for him in the squad room, looking predictably mulish and uncooperative; prepared, Casey knew, to buck anything but concrete facts. And he had few. The rest was guessing, supposition, a powerful intuition that he was on the right track. To convince Krug, he realized, he must find some logic narrow enough, unimaginative enough, to be acceptable to a mind already made up. "Just wait, Al," he began breathlessly. "Let me lay this on you before you start flakking, okay?" He sagged into his desk chair, fishing for a cigarette, but his pack of Carltons was empty. *Some days are like this. Not many, I hope.* "Okay," he said quietly, "let's try a pattern first. I'm talking about Rees and Susannah Roche, Al. Two people who might've met by accident. But whether they did or not doesn't matter. Because any time they spent together after they met wasn't accidental, right? So the next question is purpose—*why* they went *where* they went. That make sense so far?"

Krug shrugged. "You're doing the talking."

"Okay, all we've got to go on is what Rees told us. Dinner and a party. We know there *was* a party. We know the people who gave it were her partners in the counterfeiting deal. What we don't know is if Rees was part of it, but that doesn't matter either. All that matters is they went to the party for a reason. That part of the evening wasn't fun and games. So what about the other part, Al?" Casey leaned forward. "What about that boozy leisurely dinner while her million-dollar caper was coming unstuck?"

THIRTY-TWO

The neon sign he remembered was still lighted, but the parking lot looked almost empty tonight. Making a U-turn on the highway, Rees pulled into the lot, letting the Volkswagen roll across the graveled surface until it stopped from lack of momentum.

With the motor killed and the loud brittle crunching of the tires ended, the quiet seemed like sudden deafness. Then he heard the sea—not a pounding tonight, but a slow rolling murmur as subtle and pervasive as a heartbeat. But slower than his own. Uneven. Sucking in the cool salt air blowing through his open car window, he felt a collapse in himself, a change of pitch which he hoped was only a let-down from the tension of high-speed driving. But past experience had shown him the alchemy of the loser—desperation changed swiftly into helpless despair, vitality into the sluggishness which Stevens had called—

"Oh, *Christ*," he groaned aloud. Quit thinking. And quit, for God's sake, quoting Stevens to yourself. Time to move now. Time to act. Like a blind man looking for light at the end of a tunnel.

The restaurant building was two-storied, flanked on either side—Rees noticed vaguely as he approached it scuffing through the fine gravel—with two wings of fencing painted the same color as the building. The southern fence shielded what must be a large scullery and storage area—perhaps a delivery dock also— since part of the fence was hinged, forming wide double gates. The shorter section of fencing to the north had been built to close off public access to the beach. He spied above it a stairway, but no gate in the fence.

Lights burned in the upstairs windows, he saw, dim behind drawn draperies. Two rooms up there, he decided. Perhaps three. An office and a small apartment? Someone there Susannah had seen briefly. With a message, perhaps. Gossip, something. Possibly another strand in the invisible web of violence and sudden death which had caught him like a passing fly.

Opening the heavy door into the restaurant, he saw that the place was almost empty. A thin chain closed off the dining area. On it hung a hand-lettered sign saying, *Sorry no food due to kitchen disaster.* The only customers were a noisy group of drinkers at the bar. Freddy seemed to be urging them all to leave. And when he spied Rees standing in the nightclubby dimness of the foyer, he shrieked exasperatedly, "Sorry, we're closing!"

Rees headed for the stairway.

"Wait a minute, sweetie." Freddy was rushing across the bar area. "If you're looking for the—*Oh.*" Obviously recognizing Rees, he stopped. "Don't believe this," he breathed. "*What're* you *doing* here? You're—"

"Like to talk to whoever was upstairs—"

"—supposed to be—What? *What did you say?*"

"Last evening." The fool must be drunk. Repelled by the made-up masklike face, Rees smiled stiffly. "It's a private matter. So if he's there, I'll just go up if you don't mind."

But Freddy didn't move. And short of shoving him aside, Rees realized he wasn't going to get by without some sort of explanation. Try the truth? he wondered. No, too hazardous. Don't forget you're a blind man in a tunnel.

"It's about Susannah," he explained, trying to conceal his desperation. "You heard what happened?" But there was no response. "She died early this morning. A fall from her apartment—"

"*What's that got to do with us?*"

Drunk surely. And another one upstairs? Ignoring the brutal answer to Freddy's brutal question, Rees said evenly, "The police seem to think she killed herself. I didn't believe it at first. But now I think maybe she did. Anyway, it—well, it bothers me. You can understand. I'm trying to find people she talked to yester—"

"My God, a *pilg*rimage? Is *that* what you're here for?" Freddy cackled wildly. "Now I've heard—But what makes you think *we'd* know anything about it?"

"A little while after we arrived last night, I saw her talking to someone on the stairs. And since it's marked private—"

"*Did* you." Freddy's voice fell, but he was smiling brilliantly now. "Aren't we the perceptive one, though." He peered beyond Rees. "And you're alone? A lonely pilgrim." he giggled, waving airily in the direction of the stairs. "If you can find anybody to talk to, have at it, sweetie."

The short carpeted flight climbed to a small landing where the stairs turned, behind a wall, in the opposite direction. Another few steps led up to a door which stood open. Rees hesitated, then stepped into a large lamplit apartment. Windows on the west, the sea side, stood open, the draperies billowing out, giving him a glimpse of a narrow sun deck. Two inner doors to other rooms were closed. He could hear no sound of anyone moving about, but Rees was confident that someone was here. Had to be. Because, in an ashtray, a small cigar was smoldering, half smoked.

"Hello," he called. "Anybody home?"

The cigar fumed silently, fueling his prickly sense that someone was watching him. But it might be only his own apprehension, he knew, the guilty feeling of intruding into a strange and secretive world.

"Good night—good *night*," Freddy's peevish voice floated hollowly up the stairwell. Rushing closing time, Rees thought. *If you can find anybody to talk to.* Remembering Freddy's mocking cackle, he knew he'd been a fool to come here.

But too late for that now—he had to satisfy himself. His footsteps muffled by the thick carpeting, Rees moved toward the closed inner doors. The first he knocked on, then opened, let into a bathroom which was dark and smelled of aftershave. The second showed him a bedroom lit by lamps, his own image peering through the doorway reflected back by the mirrored far wall. A whorehouse bedroom, but with one difference: all the explicit nudes covering the other three walls were males.

Outside in the parking lot, car doors slammed; someone laughed shrilly. Motors roared, revved up drunkenly. Then headlights swept like beacons across the drawn draperies over the land-side windows. Rees heard a door banging downstairs—the heavy restaurant entrance, he guessed. Freddy would be up the stairs in a minute.

Crossing to the French windows, he parted the lightly blowing draperies. But the deck was empty, spume-dampened, the sea beyond shining like polished obsidian. At high tide, he thought vaguely, you could probably surf-cast from here—

"You looking for somebody?"

Turning quickly, startled by the nearness of the bulky figure behind him, Rees recognized Mr. America, the muscular narcissus of the life-sized picture hanging behind the bar downstairs. "Oh, hello," he said conventionally, his heart leaping with shock. "Sorry to barge in—" But something remote, blank-looking in the other man's face stopped him. Rees stepped back, tripping over the sill of the French doors to the sun deck. And falling heavily, he stared up into a face as pitiless as a stone god's. *Set yourself up*, Stevens's voice boomed like a bell in his mind. *Whatever it looks like, it's hopelessness.* But this is someone else's nightmare, he thought sadly. Then pile-driver fists hit him, and his mind exploded into blackness.

THIRTY-THREE

Coastal traffic was light at this hour—too early for trucks, too late for joy riders—only an occasional southbound traveler causing Casey to lower his high beams. To their right the clifflike, fragile palisades walling the land side of the highway seemed to hang over them, threatening more slides at any moment. On the sea side of the road, through occasional gaps between clusters of beach houses, the surf gleamed phosphorescent against the black. Far out to sea, a pinprick shiplight flickered.

"Fishing barge," Krug grunted. "Took the wife out there once about ten years ago. Mrs. Isaak Walton, catches her limit in an hour. Rest of the day she's bitching at me to go home. How anybody can spend a whole day fishing is beyond her—quote, unquote." His bucket seat creaked when he swiveled to face Casey, trying to peer beyond him at house numbers. "Ought to be there in a couple minutes." Casey glimpsed a dim smile. "You going to spell out the rest before we get there—or do we keep on playing your bubble game?"

So much for trying to fox your foxy uncle. Feeling like a deflated balloon, Casey slowed slightly. "While I was still at the hospital, I called that waiter. Charley. He wasn't in, but I talked to his mother again."

"Lucky you."

"She gave me the name of the chef at the restaurant. Seems he's another of Charley's favorites. Joe Cummings. Lives at Trancas."

"And?"

"He claims the restaurant stove was working fine last night. First he heard of any trouble was when Freddy called him just before he left for work."

"So what's that mean? The stove could've blown up sometime during the night."

"Okay, here's another piece. Charley's mother said she gave him our card. But he called the restaurant instead of calling us."

"So?"

"Who he talked to was the ex-female impersonator. His name's Freddy Hassler. Got a record in San Francisco—morals stuff. Description makes him about thirty, five-five, skinny build, blond."

Krug exhaled softly. "So you got it all figured out, hah? My partner, the showboat."

On a pendulum, he swung in and out of consciousness, aware only of pain at first; then of movement; then, when motion ceased, of voices muttering.

He was lying on cement, Rees realized vaguely. Lying on his side in a dark place that smelled of cooking grease and food. A kitchen?

"Get his car in first," a guttural voice very close to him said. "I'll get the truck ready."

A door opened somewhere out of Rees's view, letting in cool sea air and a strong smell of garbage. Nauseated, dizzy, he tried to turn his head away, but the bones in his neck grated agonizingly. His head pounded. His arms and legs felt paralyzed—bound tightly, he realized, at his wrists and ankles. What a fool he'd been to think this was someone else's nightmare.

From outside came a grating sound. Something heavy being dragged across gravel, Rees guessed. The wide gates in the south-side fence? This must be the restaurant kitchen, then. They had carried him down the interior stairs.

He heard a Volkswagen start, gears clashing, the jerky progress of tires across gravel. Raising himself with a stifled groan, Rees peered around the shadowy kitchen. No one here now. Both outside. He began hitching himself across the greasy floor until he was able to see out the door.

A huge shadow which he recognized as a truck blocked his view upward. He heard a wooden banging, as if someone was shifting heavy floorboards, and the whirring change of motor pitch as the Volkswagen was jockeyed back and forth again and again. His ground-level view seemed full of wheels. Two or three vehicles, he decided—the truck, the Volkswagen and another standard-sized car of some sort, all contained in the large fenced-in kitchen enclosure.

"Okay, hold it," a deep voice was saying commandingly. "Close the gate, and I'll get him."

Listening to the heavy grating sound again, the crunch of approaching footsteps, Rees struggled to free his hands. But the bonds were so tight they cut into his flesh and tendons—not a chance of loosening them, he realized. And the big man coming for him. So play possum then? But they would realize he had moved, he thought desperately. Got to get back there. If he had a chance at all, it would be in waiting to see what happened.

Scrabbling frantically, he inched himself backward across the greasy cement as far as he could. Then he lay rigid on his side, willing himself to relax as someone bent over him breathing hard. He felt hands under his shoulders and knees. Hands as big as mitts, as hard as iron. Then he was lifted like a child and carried out.

Head spinning, Rees risked a glimpse through slitted lids—a truck opened to receive cargo, two boards slanting like a runway into the truck bed from the ground. And positioned to be loaded was his Volkswagen, passenger door open, Freddy behind the wheel. Someone else's nightmare. And he saw now its pattern.

Struggling frantically, Rees opened his mouth to yell. But before he could, steely fingers clamped his throat shut. And he knew this time he was dying.

"—Timing more than anything makes it hang together, Al. I'm just guessing, but what I think happened is this: by the time they got the U-Haul stashed, something went wrong. Otherwise they would've dumped the stuff and got rid of the truck."

"What makes you think they didn't? Same deal as the Mercedes maybe. Stashed it in a garage someplace."

"Then why the delay, Al? Why wait four or five hours to kill the Godwins?" And four or five hours after that, he thought, to make the anonymous call. "Whatever happened, I've got a feeling time may be short, Al." Feeling like Scheherazade, Casey increased his speed as smoothly as an old lady's chauffeur. "If they were pinned down. You see what I mean? And they got panicky—?"

"Yeah, I see all right." Krug was peering through the windshield. "Looks like the slide's just about cleared away." Then he turned, glaring at Casey. "So what kept 'em after the road crews split?"

"Business, Al."

"The hell it did. Look there"—he was pointing—"their neon sign's out."

"That's what I meant about time being short. They were open less than an hour ago."

"Pull up across the road. *Pull up, goddam you*—I'm not running into no buzz saw without some backup units behind me!"

Using the Mustang's motor compression to brake, Casey shifted down and doused his headlights, rolling to a silent stop across the highway from the restaurant. The building was dark, he saw. Except for a dim glow—possibly a nightlight—emanating from the large fenced enclosure to the south. The tarpulin-covered, shedlike outline looming over the fence which he had noticed earlier seemed more clearly defined than he remembered.

Then he realized why: the tarp must be gone. And what it had covered was not crates, a shed, or building materials. Casey knew now that his sense of urgency had been correct.

Crimping the wheel, he floored the accelerator, roaring across the highway in front of an oncoming car. Krug's howling protest was drowned by the machine-gun rattle of gravel pellets under the fenders as they streaked across the parking lot. Casey flicked on the high beams, then stood on the brake. The silhouette, silvery and three-dimensional now, was the top of an aluminum truck with orange-painted lettering barely visible over the fence: *U-Haul.*

Krug leaped out, stumbling, while the Mustang was still sliding broadside beyond the closed fence gate. "*Police,*" he roared. "Come out with your hands up!"

There was no answer, no sound at all except the pulsing of the sea and the Mustang's idling. Krug shoved at the gates where they came together, but the two wings held solid. Peering through the crack between them, he shook his head. "Can't see a damn thing."

"I'll try the other side, Al. There's a stairway—"

Krug was pounding on the heavy restaurant door by this time. "Talk about foul-ups. You and your goddam solo acts!"

There was no access to the stair Casey could spy above the northside fence. Obviously it led down to the beach. "Have to climb this, I guess."

"Yeah, you do that. And if it's the wrong U-Haul, we'll have sixteen wop lawyers—*What's that?*"

Wood scraping on wood. "Al, the gate—"

But Krug was already in motion, sprinting heavily along the front of the building. Casey caught up with him just as a starter whirred and a heavy motor boomed, backfiring. Krug grabbed him. "Watch it!" Then a splintering crash deafened them.

Both gates exploded open, the wing nearest Krug and Casey scything the air like a projectile, slamming against the stationary part of the fence with such force that the thick boards cracked open. Exhaust billowing behind it, a truck shot out, slewing across the parking lot, spraying sheets of gravel. Tires screeching on the pavement, it rocked onto the highway, swinging north while, simultaneously inside the enclosure, another vehicle started up.

Against all regulation procedure, Krug jumped into the sudden blinding glare of headlights, taking a target-shooting stance—feet apart, Detective Special firm in both hands at nearly arm's length. "Police officer," he was yelling. "Douse those lights!"

There was a moment when nothing happened, and covering his partner, Casey shouted a warning. Then the headlights went out. He began to breathe again.

"All right, out of there," Krug yelled. "*Move* it!"

The door on the driver's side of the Dodge van inside the enclosure opened, and moving with glacial slowness, a dim figure climbed out.

"Lean against the side there. Against the door—*move* it! That's right. Hands out wide. Feet out—"

The driver was smallish and wiry, with long blond hair. Twitching with nerves as Casey frisked him. Smelling of fear-sweat and a potent aftershave lotion. Except for a soft groan when Casey snapped the handcuffs on him, he kept silent, refusing to answer any questions about where the truck was headed.

"Go after it," Krug told Casey grimly. "I'll handle this fruitcake."

"No, wait a minute, sweetie"—the driver's wavering, scared voice followed Casey as he ran to his idling Mustang—"you're making an awful mistake—"

Gravel flying like buckshot behind him, Casey roared out of the parking lot, swinging northward onto the highway. No sign of the truck ahead. But with only a five-minute lead, he knew, his chances of catching it were good. The only escape routes off the highway were infrequent canyon roads leading into the hills.

At the first, Topanga Canyon, he swung into a lighted gas station, skidding to a stop on the cement apron between the pumps and the glass-walled station office. "Police," he yelled through the open door at the attendant sitting inside. "You see a U-Haul truck pass in the last few minutes?"

"Yeah, and driving like a loony!" Grinning, the attendant pointed right, toward the canyon road. "Took that rig around the corner on two—"

"Call the Sheriff's station right away. Tell them all units to a restaurant called the Ultimate Perception. You got that?"

"Ultimate—yeah, I got it. Hey, what's—?"

"And tell them a U-Haul truck on Topanga Canyon Road. They'll know what it's about when they get to the restaurant."

Casey gunned away again, streaking up the curving grade which, as it climbed into the mountains towering between the sea and San Fernando Valley, became a sinuous nightmare of switchback cornering. A Grand Prix course at almost any speed, suicidal if you pushed it. But if he was to catch the U-Haul truck, he had to.

THIRTY-FOUR

Agony from the constant jolting roused him. A snoring sound. His own breathing, Rees realized dimly. Long snorting suckings of air through his nostrils. Because his mouth was sealed shut.

He opened his eyes—thought he opened them, lids lifting, a sense of seeing—but he was utterly blind. Or blindfolded. Trying to feel if it were so, he was reminded that his wrists were tied. His ankles also. Painfully twisting one wrist so that he could investigate, he felt his face, confirming tape over his mouth, sweat-sticky cheeks, nose, quivering eyelids—no blindfold. So this pitching, disorienting darkness was the inside of some moving sealed-in place? In his confusion, prison horror stories of solitary punishment holes blazed up, terrifyingly real. He closed his eyes, trying to will himself into unconsciousness again.

But his brain would not sleep. A stubborn perception of life stirred in him, and with it, a dim hope. With numb fingers, he worked at the tape over his mouth, finally loosening it enough so that he could breathe freely. It was comfort for a time: lying cramped and aching, he gulped in air greedily. Then molelike, cautious, he began to investigate as much as his bound hands would permit. The seat he lay on felt like leather. A split seat. No, it was Naugahyde, he decided. His half-dead fingertips gave back other tactile recognitions: glass, knobs, pedals, a slanting column topped by a wheel. A steering wheel. And everything familiar: the Volkswagen. Driverless, vehicle in a lunatic nightmare, it was roaring through black nothingness.

His headlights punching out the darkness seemed to pull Casey's Mustang, dragging it wildly around curve after curve, a giant child's toy. At every outside corner arc, his rear wheels drifted, the chassis fishtailing as he compensated, pitching like a cowboy tied to a crazy bronc. Flashing glimpses of houses reeled by, signs saying *For Rent* and *Speed Kills,* brushy hillsides, clumps of live oak, steep gullies which his lights jumped eerily, creating the optical illusion that he was flying.

Speed kills. Climbing up and up the dark mountainside, Casey risked a look now and then to see if he could spot any lights ahead on the switchback turns. Speed may kill the killer, too. No such luck. But a truck going at this rate—The hell, he thought, nuts like that one lead charmed lives. Only policemen and other mortals suffer consequences.

Light flickered ahead, for one moment fooling him. Then Casey realized it must be Topanga Village—a modest shopping center which probably enjoyed a bit of community nighttime illumination. A minute later, as he boomed by stores and a startled hippie couple walking on the roadside, his guess was confirmed. Beyond lay another sharp curve. As his tires howled, he was presented with the sudden choice of two roads—the one he was on or Old Topanga Road, which forked to the left. Did the two join again later? He couldn't remember, and it was too late to worry about it.

All around him now was what looked to be a real wilderness—an illusion, he knew, for the area was a network of dirty side roads leading to mountain hideaways and tiny so-called ranches. Any one of them might serve as a bolt hole for the truck. But only the steeliest sort of fugitive would try such a trick. If he did, Sheriff's units would catch him on the way down again. Maybe.

Neon-paint letters six feet high—*GRACIOUS COUNTRY LIVING*—caught his headlights. Retaining a surreal retinal image from the sign—a giant couple embracing in front of a palatial home—Casey realized he must be approaching a new real estate development. Some subdivider racing to beat the ecologists, he decided. By next year what was left of this mountain area must surely be designated parkland.

He could see the tops of the mountains now, rounded, folded black velvet against the hazy midnight-blue of the sky. Only a few more miles and the vast panorama of the San Fernando Valley would be spread out below him. All downhill grade from then on, a free-wheeling curving deathtrap. Casey pounded the wheel. Damn, *damn*. Either the truck had ducked somewhere—

He saw it then: two winking red coals which for an instant became one as a vehicle disappeared around the curve ahead. Taillights. Behind Casey's eyes, a pulse began thumping. Let it be the truck. Let it. Screeching around the sheer rock cut which walled the inside of the curve, he held his breath, waiting for his wheeling headlights to show him. But there was another curve ahead, something silvery disappearing just as his high beams caught it.

Rocking wildly through the turn, the Mustang began to drift leftward, and Casey eased the wheel over, watching the emptiness of a hundred-foot gully sliding toward him. Be like flying, he thought, hypnotized, and for one tick of his blood a thrill-temptation scorched his mind. Then instinct and training took over, sensing the end of the drift. Steering right again, he gunned on the uphill straightaway. Less than a quarter of a mile ahead, shining like sheet silver, he could see the truck, read the orange lettering: *U-HAUL*, and below that, *Adventure In Moving.*

With no hope of response, Casey flicked his lights, signaling. And as if in answer, black puffs of carbon exhaust billowed from the truck. Accelerating, Casey pushed the Mustang closer and closer, planning to draw abreast of the truck and herd it into the next narrow lay-by cut into the right-hand hillside. But as he started to draw up beside the truck, it reeled toward him suddenly. "Oh, *beau*tiful," he yelled, "*very* hincty," and he stood on his brake, watching fascinated as the rear of the truck missed the front of the Mustang by no more than a couple of inches.

So the game was to be Chicken. Between a truck and a passenger car? No game at all on a mountain road, Casey decided. One near miss and he could clearly calculate how easily he might be bounced off into the sheer-sided gully to the left. So pursuit then, he thought. Push the bastard till he either cracks up, or that U-Haul finally craps out.

But the driver of the truck chose another alternative.

THIRTY-FIVE

H is Volkswagen was a hearse, Rees realized now. A hearse carried piggyback complete with corpse-to-be. He would be found somewhere like the motorcyclist. Bottom of a cliff, probably. Another accident case. FUGITIVE DIES IN MISHAP. And investigating police would find—

The gun, the *gun*. Jerking upright, bracing himself against the steering wheel, he tried to manipulate the door handle, but his numb fingers would not work. His hands and feet felt like alien putty. Must find something, he thought feverishly. Anything that might saw through the wrist bindings.

No, light first, he thought. Fumbling in the jolting blackness, he found the headlight switch on the dashboard. The sudden blinding brilliance of the aluminum truck interior was agonizing at first and then merciful. To see again was to live again.

Scrambling out of the Volkswagen, Rees found that he could not stand, so he knelt beside the car, searching under and behind the seats. But the gun was gone. A wave of blackness engulfed him, and he slumped on the reeling floor of the truck. Hopeless. But the blessed glare of his headlights made a lie of his fatalism. Somehow he must untie himself. Or cut free? Time was probably short on to. Trying to picture what might aid him from the glove compartment, he suddenly remembered his sunglasses. Plastic lenses, had to be. But breakable. And anything that breaks makes a cutting edge.

For one breath-held moment as he whirled around the corner, Casey believed he had lost the truck; it must have plunged into the gully. To the right a huge billboard rushed at him, *GRACIOUS COUNTRY LIVING*, a repetition of the one he'd seen before. A banner across the bottom said *Open October*. This was the entrance to the subdivision: skinned hillsides, snowy-white concrete avenues already laid out, acres of houses in various skeletal stages of framing. The truck had turned in.

Passing the billboard which had hidden the U-Haul for a moment, Casey shot between pretentious gateposts, careening into a turnaround with a palm tree island in the center. Then he streaked after the bobbing taillights. So the game wasn't to be Chicken after all, he guessed, but Hide and Seek? A duel of driving skill, *mano a mono*. Okay, he thought. *Okay*.

The spotless concrete streets curved gracefully, following the rolling contours of the hilltops—climbing, dipping, a confusing cat's cradle he could get lost in fast, Casey knew, unless he tailed the truck as closely as possible. Feeding power to the already roaring motor, he kept narrowing the distance from the twinkling red dots. Then suddenly they went out. On two wheels, the truck dodged into a branching narrow avenue—a continuous turn, like a cloverleaf, which disappeared behind a knoll.

Afraid of losing his advantage, Casey spun into the corkscrew turn, fighting the wheel. Then he spied the U-Haul ahead. But it was going the wrong way. Oh wow, oh mother, the bastard's going to ram! Blinded by the sudden flaring headlights through his windshield, he jerked the wheel right, bouncing up over the curb, slewing into a wild spin which sent a pile of lumber flying. His tires, trying to find traction on the soft graded surface, spun, whipping the chassis. And hanging onto the wheel, Casey caught a dizzy glimpse of a monstrous looming shadow bearing down on him. Mountain to Mahomet, he thought crazily. Sandbagged.

Inside the truck, Rees had been sawing frantically at the cord cutting into his left wrist, the piece of broken plastic lens clamped in the numb fingers of his right hand, his arm through the spoke of the steering wheel to keep from being flung to and fro. Each lurch of the truck made him miss and slice himself. His left wrist was bloody as raw meat. But he could feel a loosening, a tingling as his constricted veins once more fed feeling to his hand. Just one free and he could untie himself. One minute more, he thought. Then suddenly weightless, he was lifted and flung like a puppet against the Volkswagen's windshield.

The soaring sensation of weightlessness caught Casey, too, as the passenger side of the Mustang caved in, glass shattering, and the car heeled over, skidding on two wheels into the scattered pile of lumber. His head hit the window frame beside him. One of his headlights burst with a gunshot explosion. In the lopsided light left to him, he glimpsed the truck through a cloud of radiant dust. Hunter now, not the hunted. But if he could reach the pavement, he'd have the advantage of greater maneuverability. Casey gunned the motor. But his tires kept spinning. The Mustang was a trap now, he realized, and a second before the truck hit him again, he jumped out, feeling something snap as he landed, tumbling through dirt and broken glass and smashed lumber.

Only vaguely aware of the warm trickling on his forehead, Rees lay dazed, half in, half out of the Volkswagen, which was shifting unsteadily now, brakes creaking as it rocked this way and that. His hands were free, he discovered, the wrist binding having snapped where he had been sawing at it. Crouching, he tore wildly at the knot at his ankles, finally loosening it enough to pull one foot free. Then he staggered to the loading doors. But there was no way to open them from inside.

The second impact threw him against the side of the truck and then to the floor. Gasping for the breath that had been knocked out of him, Rees watched the Volkswagen's jolting changes of position. Sooner or later it might crush him, he realized. Like a battering ram. But what can kill might also save? Like fire, he told himself. Like water. For God's sake, take a chance.

Pushing himself upright again, he clung to the car, reaching in to check that the gearshift lever was in neutral. Then he released the hand brake and plastered himself against the side of the truck, waiting.

Pain in his right arm half paralyzed Casey, and for an instant stunned, he watched his Mustang rearing through the clouds of dust at a crazy angle. Metal ground on metal, rending. In the U-Haul's headlights, shards of glass flew like crystalline rain. Then a living thing, mindless, raging, the truck roared around the wreckage, straight at him through the swirling dust.

All the things he had depended on were useless now— badge, gun, two-ton car. But an armored man, he thought as he ran dodging, is the prisoner of his armor. His own shadow leaped enormously long ahead of him as the headlights gained. Prisoner, his mind repeated back at him insanely. Prisoner? Stopping abruptly, he turned and faced into the white glare. Oh, Jesus, so *close*. His flesh shrinking in dread against his fragile bones, he waited, cradling his broken arm. And when the truck was almost upon him—he could see the space between the front wheels, the height underneath—he flung himself into the dirt, praying as the front tires rumbled by on either side of his head that he was flat enough for the drainpan and drive axle to clear his body.

Sound battered him. Fountains of dirt half buried him. For the space of a heartbeat, Casey was not sure he had survived. Then the truck was gone, and choking on dust, he jumped up, seeing the red blaze of brake lights as the truck skidded. Something crashed inside the aluminum body, and risking a quick look as it swung about, accelerating, he saw the loading doors bulging outward. Then suddenly they burst open and light streamed out. Unbelieving, Casey saw a blue Volkswagen emerging weirdly slow, back wheels dropping off the truck bed, the underside of the body grinding as the chassis slid over the tailgate, hung there for a moment, then bounced off with a clang of shock absorbers and punished springs.

But the truck did not stop. Casey was pinned like a moth in the high beams which sought out every stone, twig, heap of building materials, casting immense, eerie moonscape shadows. His .38 was useless, he knew, unless he could duck somewhere long enough to brace his left arm and take accurate aim. Peashooter against an elephant. But if he could hit a tire. Dreamer, dreamer. He'd be hamburger unless he could find a hiding place immediately.

The Volkswagen seemed to career away in the darkness, headlights bobbing, tires squashing—an illusion, Rees knew: it was the truck which was moving. Again in darkness, he crouched near the flapping loading doors, and when the one nearest him swung wide, he jumped. He lit hard, rolling over and over to lie stunned in the soft dirt. But alive, alive. Sky above him. Smell of sumac, openness, wonderful space—but still caught in the nightmare.

He saw the wreckage of the car first, a man running for it gnomelike but strangely familiar in the blanching whiteness of headlights. The man dodged behind the wrecked car. And as the headlights bore down on it, Rees saw a spat of flame, heard the crack of a gunshot. Then the truck hit the wreck, and with a roar the crippled Mustang exploded. In the hellish glare, Rees saw a shadow leaping from the cab of the truck.

Casey saw it, too. No hiding now. With no hope of hitting anything, he fired left-handed again and again. But the huge figure, an evil *djinn* out of the orange-yellow crackling glare, kept coming at him. *Either a maniac or some muscle type as strong as a gorilla.* "Police," he roared. "Freeze!" Then the giant shadow sprang at him, and gripped by pain, terror, rage, Casey went down. His gun flew. Tumbling, grappling helplessly, he had a wheeling glimpse of something at the edge of the leaping light. A man. Blue Volkswagen. My God, his mind made the connection, *Rees?* "Help," he yelled. *"Help me."*

But Rees only stood there.

Blind man in a tunnel. Running man. And in his mind she kept laughing. Falling. Laughing. *What you can't see—*

But in the red-hot unearthly light from the burning car, he saw it very clearly, gleaming like a snake in the whirling dust. *Keep living dangerously.* He scooped up the gun. *Keep living.*

Whatever happened from now on, he knew he was through running.

THIRTY-SIX

"What a *scene*," Krug hooted, no respecter of hospital quiet. His voice seemed to explode inside Casey's head. "Looked like the end of a war up there on that goddam hill! Mustang's burning. U-Haul's burning. Volkswagen's sitting there with three flats and the headlights on. You're laying there maybe dead in the dirt. And if that ain't enough, there's for Chrissake *Rees*, playing King of the Mountain with your .38!"

A wanted ex-con in possession of a policeman's gun. Feeling suddenly sick, Casey stared at him. Between his shout for help and waking up in the ambulance was utter darkness: no one knew perhaps that Rees had saved him—

"Talk about showdowns," Krug was saying, obviously relishing his story. "For a while there I figured we hit the granddaddy of 'em all—"

"Al, what happened? With Rees, I mean."

"Ah, hell, what d'you think?"

"He got roughed up a bit, that's all," Lieutenant Timms said soothingly from a corner. "Nothing a couple ice packs and a steam bath won't cure." He smiled as Casey sank back into the pillows again. "Don't worry, we've got him pretty well pegged now."

"That's for sure," Krug agreed enigmatically. "Anyhow, like I was saying, it's showdown time, see. We got Freddy stashed in one of the Sheriff's units. And by this time he's shaking like a bowl of jelly. He takes one look at Rees and his boyfriend, and, man, does that fruitcake start talking!"

"Russo—that's the big one—hasn't done any yet," Timms took up the story. "But we've got everything we need from the other one, Hassler." He peered at Casey. "How's the arm, by the way? The orthopedic guy said no complications expected."

"Thanks, he already told me, sir. I'll be out of here tomorrow." As he yawned helplessly, the burning wreck blazed up in Casey's mind, a troubling vision of Rees as a fiery, unaiding, somehow judgmental spirit. If he had not shouted for help, he wondered, would he be dead by now? More than ever, he was aware of the mysterious opacity of human behavior—

"Seems we figured it right," Timms was saying. "The girl put the whole caper together. She met Barrett at one of those disco joints on the Sunset Strip. Last November. They spent the night together—which was all it took to open up a boob like Barrett. The next day she nailed those two restaurant characters with the big scheme. Then she lined up Godwin. They all met once to put it together, and from then on the girl was the go-between."

"Only one fly in the ointment"—Krug was grinning—"Godwin's wife. Jealous, can you beat it? Her husband's out knocking off a partner yet, and all she worries about is he's out all night with another woman."

"Well, that's Freddy's version, she may have another story." But Timms looked as if he believed this one. "Seems she didn't know the night of the party what they'd been up to the night before. Evidently she must've found the black hat ditched in the Renault—anyway, wherever Godwin stashed it when he transferred it from the Mercedes. Rees saw her blowing her top to Roche about it. Nobody but Roche and Godwin knew then it was a piece of red-hot evidence. Rees is lucky they didn't waste him for seeing it."

"So Godwin was the hit-and-run driver?" Aware that his mind was dragging, Casey struggled to focus. "Then he was the one who searched Rees's room."

"Right." Timms nodded. "What he thought he'd accomplish nobody knows. Maybe he only meant to scare Rees off. But when he found those parole papers—" He made an offering gesture. "Pure gold if he could think how to use 'em. Anyway, he must've passed on the news to Roche, because she told the two at the restaurant later. Guess they figured Rees might turn out to be their ace in the hole."

Nobody mentioned that he almost had been.

Timms kept chewing his lip, frowning into space. "Looks to me like their big trouble all along was the right hand never knowing what the left was up to. For instance, the two restaurant guys didn't know till Monday that Barrett had blown their deal. Godwin and the girl were afraid to tell 'em, scared they'd call it off—so Freddy claims. So instead of warning everybody, winding things up and getting the hell out, they staged their phony accident in the alley. But Monday night when she took Rees to the restaurant, she spilled the beans."

"Smart broad probably figured she was covering all bases," Krug said. "Didn't I tell you it was a natural she outsmarted herself?"

"Russo was wise enough to track down the Mercedes right away," Timms continued. "He was the so-called brother who phoned the old man Barrett rented the garage from. And once he knew we had the Mercedes—well, you can figure the rest. Probably guessed we could connect Barrett with the girl sooner or later. Time for another accident." He leaned against the hospital bed, yawning. "Where they really went wrong was trying to have it both ways. Typical amateurs," he added contemptuously. "Pros would've had a getaway plan worked out in case they needed it. But these clucks figured they could have the whole banana—a quarter of a million each, tax-free, nary a problem. Let six months or so pass after the paper's peddled. Godwin and Russo sell their businesses. Off they go, scot-free, thumbing their noses at the law."

But instead, one thing had led to another. Casey kept blinking, trying to make the connections. But his brain felt like a mass of soggy cotton. "It's the timing today that really bugs me—"

"Yesterday, you mean." Krug jerked a thumb toward the window letting in gray dawn light. "It's tomorrow, Sleeping Beauty."

Another day. Casey thought he had never seen anything as beautiful as that misty, shadowless, silken light from which tomorrow was emerging like a dream realized. "What I can't figure—if they were going to do it—why they waited so long to kill the Godwins. Something else unexpected must've happened. Besides the slide, I mean."

"We happened." Krug laughed at Casey's expression. "Yeah, you and me, sport. With the help of that waiter we never laid an eye on."

"But...Oh." Casey saw it suddenly. "Charley tipped them we were checking on—what did I say? 'A couple that had dinner there the night before'?"

Krug nodded. "According to Freddy, they figured we were getting closer. Too close, anyway, with that truck sitting there. And they're ready to flip anyway, what with the slide—meaning an audience of twenty road crew guys if they try to get the U-Haul out."

"But the Godwins," Casey reminded him.

"More trail-covering, according to Freddy. They were scared we'd get to them next, and the Godwins'd blow it. Freddy says he called 'em to see if we'd been there yet. They said maybe, but they were laying low. That was about three-thirty, four. Half an hour later, Russo pays 'em a fast call—"

"Christ, we had it straight from the horse's mouth," Timms broke in disgustedly. " 'Something or somebody was ready,' remember? Only what the Godwin woman was trying to say was 'Freddy,' not 'ready.' If we'd used our heads—"

Another near miss.

But it didn't seem to bother Krug. "Okay, Russo knocks off the Godwins," he went on. "Then he stops by Rees's motel long enough to stash the murder gun in his Volkswagen. Incidentally," he interrupted himself, "Rees was our mysterious visitor, would you believe it? This is a guy that's gonna fall in the shit no matter what. Stupid bastard claims he was so scared we wouldn't believe it was accidental he found 'em that he couldn't think straight. Won't admit it, of course, but what I figure is, he ran as fast as he could. Then he found the gun in his car about ten. Guess it scared him enough to get him back on the track again."

"Some track," Timms grunted. "Instead of reporting it to us, he walks right into the snakepit." He blew out his breath. "Amateurs. They're the real policeman's nightmare, not the crooks. But we should've figured out the red herring angle," he added as if he had invented the expression. "Why the possibility didn't occur to us with that phony anonymous call—" He shook his head. "What comes of getting locked in on one idea, right?"

"Right," Krug agreed solemnly. "Got to keep an open mind in this business, that's for sure."

With the promise of three full days off, and at least a month of day-tour desk work to be assigned until the cast was off his arm, Casey fell asleep, smiling. Thirty beautiful nights free ahead. Surely time enough for even a one-armed lover? It was sweet-dream time. The sweetest. Visions of reconciliation and romantic advancement—

But he had slept only an hour, Casey discovered when he was wakened for breakfast. And he had another visitor.

"I'm on my way to the Parole Authority," Paul Rees said awkwardly. "Thought I'd drop by first and thank you."

"Seems to me it should be the other way around." Casey studied the sallow, exhausted face. Something concealed there still, he thought. But Rees was a man who would always harbor ghosts. "Aren't you starting out kind of early for a nine o'clock appointment?"

"Probably. But I don't know how long it might take to get my Volks out of the garage. The police garage," he added stiffly. "They—you—impounded it. But I was told I could get a release in a little while."

They chatted in a half-friendly but cautious fashion for a bit. Then suddenly reminded, Casey said, "About that money. Doesn't matter, but I'm still curious. Did you really win it in a poker game?"

God, Rees thought, don't they ever quit? A policeman is a policeman is a policeman. He was not out of danger yet. "Let's just say I won it, period. The details belong to a time I'd like to forget about forever."

"Fair enough," Casey started to say, but the phone on the stand beside his hospital bed rang. Joey, he thought. It's ESP. But nothing so mysterious, it was his mother: What on earth had happened to him? Was he all right? She hadn't been able to get a single sensible word out of those men he worked with, so Dad had called the captain—

"Oh, *no*," Casey groaned. But he couldn't help laughing.

He was still laughing as Rees signaled good-bye and slid out into the long, waxy hospital corridor busy with attendants wheeling carts full of breakfast trays. A disembodied voice kept paging doctors. Nurses rustled by Rees as if he were invisible. Another closed world, he thought. Like prison. Like the courtroom he would be appearing in soon to testify against murderous strangers. Like the jail cell he might still occupy today if he were not lucky—

And he knew he was not when he pushed out into the cool gray morning and saw Krug lounging against an official-looking car parked at the curb.

"No answer at the Pelican, so I figured you might be here." He opened the front passenger door of the car. "Want a lift?" He grinned as Rees shook his head no. "Come on," he said derisively, "what're you scared of? Better than hoofing it to the garage, ain't it?"

Knowing he had no choice, Rees climbed into the car, his exhaustion becoming despair as he looked at the radio equipment, the rifle clamped under the dashboard, the clipboard holding lists of wanted cars and other police bulletins. The plastic bag containing the pistol had been found in the Volkswagen's trunk and impounded with the car as evidence. Evidence which someone—Krug probably—had reexamined. And a bloodhound like Krug would not miss the significance of those pieces of shoe-box lid, like a jigsaw puzzle, spelling out parole conditions broken—

"Y'know something really bugs me," Krug was saying as he pulled jerkily away from the curb. "About that scene up on the hill?" He glanced at Rees. "How come a guy like you makes a grandstand play like that? I mean, look"—he seemed to be arguing with himself—"here's a ten-ton killer about to waste a cop. No skin off yours if he does, right? Only makes it easier for you to get away, save your own neck. But instead, you mix in like a—" he broke off, laughing. "That's what bugs me! You playing hero. It just don't figure with a guy as easy to scare as you."

"Maybe you've been reading me wrong, Sergeant."

"The hell I have."

Rees stared blindly out the window. "Well, even a rat fights when it's cornered," he said bleakly.

"That's what I'm talking about, fella. You wasn't cornered up there."

"So I'm a different sort of rat. Something new for your book."

"Yeah, that's for sure. Something real new." Krug swung into an alley and stopped the car abruptly. "Okay, this is it." And again He grinned at Rees's reaction. "See what I mean? Easy to scare." He shook his head sadly, plunging his hand into his pocket.

Expecting a gun, brass knuckles—anything but what appeared—Rees flinched back against the door. Then numb with shock, he stared at the two pieces of cardboard which Krug had flipped at him. Buff shoe-box cardboard with small black printing. Put together, the two pieces spelled out *Stateline, Nevada*.

"Garage is half a block down," Krug was saying. "I signed the release, so all you got to do is receipt it and split." He leaned across Rees, opening the car door. "They'll charge you for three inner tubes, but the labor for changing the tires is on us. So we're even-steven, right?"

Rees climbed dazedly out and the door slammed behind him. Before he could turn, Krug had gunned away. *Even-steven*, the harsh voice kept echoing in his head as Rees watched the City of Santa Monica departmental car roll down the alley and disappear. Meaning debt paid. Game over. He looked at the two ragged pieces of cardboard shoe box in his hand. Then very slowly he shredded them into confetti which he scattered behind him as he walked down the alley. In two hours he was due at Parole. And with any luck, his new parole officer might be someone he could talk to...

ABOUT THE AUTHOR

 Carolyn Weston grew up in Hollywood dur-
ing the Depression. Hollywood Boulevard
was the scene of her truancies; movie houses
one refuge, the public library another. She
spent part of World War II working in an
aircraft plant, and afterward gypsied around
the country, working at anything and every-
thing (Reno gambling club, specialty wallpaper house as decora-
tor, New Orleans nightclub, Prentice-Hall and Lord and Taylor
in New York, among others!). All this time she had been writing
and discarding manuscripts, until at last one of the novels was
published. Now she lives in California.

Printed by Libri Plureos GmbH in Hamburg,
Germany